STILL WATERS

ALSO BY EMMA CARLSON BERNE

Hard to Get

STILL WATERS

Emma Carlson Berne

SIMON PULSE

NEW YORK   LONDON   TORONTO   SYDNEY

SIMON PULSE

An imprint of Simon & Schuster Children's Publishing Division

1230 Avenue of the Americas, New York, NY 10020

First Simon Pulse paperback edition December 2011

Copyright © 2011 by Emma Berne

All rights reserved, including the right of reproduction in whole or in part in any form.

SIMON PULSE, and colophon are registered trademarks of Simon & Schuster, Inc.

For information about special discounts for bulk purchases, please contact Simon & Schuster Special Sales at 1-866-506-1949 or business@simonandschuster.com.

The Simon & Schuster Speakers Bureau can bring authors to your live event. For more information or to book an event contact the Simon & Schuster Speakers Bureau at 1-866-248-3049 or visit our website at www.simonspeakers.com.

Designed by Karina Granda

The text of this book was set in Caslon.

Manufactured in the United States of America

2 4 6 8 10 9 7 5 3 1

Library of Congress Cataloging-in-Publication Data

Berne, Emma Carlson.

Still waters / by Emma Carlson Berne. — 1st Simon Pulse pbk. ed.

p. cm.

Summary: When seventeen-year-old Hannah and her eighteen-year-old boyfriend sneak off to a broken-down old cottage at a deserted lake for the weekend, things do not go at all as planned.

ISBN 978-1-4424-2114-1 (pbk.) — ISBN 978-1-4424-2115-8 (eBook)

[1. Recovered memory—Fiction. 2. Horror stories.] I. Title.

PZ7.B455139St 2011

[Fic]—dc22   2010053303

For Holly, my friend and companion

CHAPTER 1

Hannah Taylor leaned her finger on the doorbell of Colin's house, listening to the silvery chimes echo inside the sprawling Victorian. The July sun was setting behind her, firing the sky orange and lending a soft pink glow to the stone and clapboard house.

No answer. Her boyfriend's shiny Ford pickup was parked in the driveway, so he had to be home. Colin had even told her to stop by after dinner. Hannah rang again and tried the door. Locked. She pressed her face against the side window, but all she could see was the darkened foyer. Finally she tipped up a flowerpot of pansies at the corner of the porch. There was a key taped to the bottom. She unlocked the door and stepped into the Oriental-carpeted foyer. Over her head, a vaulted ceiling soared to the second story. The downstairs lights were off, and the purple twilight shadows filtered through the windows.

Hannah set the spare key down on the antique farmhouse

table cluttered with piles of mail. "Hello?" she called into the quiet. There was a rustle and a thump from the back of the house. Hannah's heart gave a little skip. "Colin?" she called again. She padded into the darkened dining room.

Suddenly the foyer blazed into light. Hannah squeezed her eyes shut against the glare. When she opened them, Colin Byrd was standing in the doorway, his hand on the light switch. His hair was rumpled and a book dangled from his hand. "Oh, hi. I fell asleep."

Hannah exhaled and went over to embrace him. "It's so dark in here." She followed him back into the den, where the deep suede couch still held the imprint of his body. She flopped down on the couch, leaning her head against the back. Colin put his book on the coffee table and stretched out on the floor, interlocking his fingers behind his head.

"My mom and dad went to some cocktail thing. How was dinner with the fam?" he asked. He started doing sit-ups.

Hannah blew out her lips. "Fine. The usual. Just me and David."

"Did you cook?"

She nodded. "Tuna casserole this time. I should teach David how to make it. Ten is old enough to cook, right?" She rocked her head back and forth, feeling the kinks in her neck. "My mom had to stay late. Cleaning up the stockroom." Her mother's new job at a big chain bookstore had great benefits, but it also meant that she worked about fifty hours a week and was rarely home before nine.

"Nineteen, twenty," Colin counted. "What's David doing?" He switched to crunches.

Hannah leaned forward and grabbed the book Colin had set down. It was a big volume of black-and-white photos. "I told him he could watch a movie after his homework was done." She paged through some shots of factories from the 1940s. "Where'd you get this?"

Colin looked over from his prone position on the carpet. "Oh, it's great. I checked it out from the library. Look at this one." He sat down next to her on the sofa. Hannah felt her pulse increase at the warmth of his body next to hers. Even after a whole year of being together.

Hannah thought of the very first day she saw Colin, at the beginning of her junior year, alone in the art room at school, holding a strip of negatives up to the light. She'd stood across the room, forgetting the ink drawing she was supposed to be putting on Mr. Walter's desk. Instead her eyes were riveted to the play of the muscles in his broad shoulders, and the span of his big-knuckled hands holding the film. Then a group of obnoxious guys had passed by the hall, the big, bluff types who seemed to take up all the air in the hallways when they swaggered by on the way to classes.

"Colin!" a big blond guy in a Yankees cap had called in. "Get your ass out here!"

Hannah's heart sank. He was one of them.

Colin wheeled around, and his face was momentarily angry. Then, as Hannah watched, he laid the negatives down with a resigned sigh and headed toward the door. Hannah wasn't surprised he hadn't noticed her on the other side of the room. She'd perfected being invisible since freshman year. But just before he left the room, he turned around and met her eyes squarely.

Her breath caught. And then he'd been gone.

Now, Hannah smiled at the memory and gazed at her boyfriend's bright blond head, which was bent over the book as he flipped through the pages.

She examined the picture he pointed out. "Cool lines in this one." But Colin didn't answer, and she looked up. He was watching her and his earnest expression made her stomach clench in anticipation. He was going to say it again.

"Hannah, I love you." His voice held just the slightest pleading note.

Hannah's fingers tightened on the book spread across her lap. She gazed down at it. "I know," she mumbled. A panoramic shot of Detroit stared up at her.

A little silence stretched between them. She heard him swallow. "You still can't say it? I thought, maybe you'd had time to think it over by now."

Hannah rose to her feet abruptly, and the book slid splayed onto the carpet. She crossed the room to the upright piano and tapped out "This Old Man." She focused on her fingers pressing each shiny key so she wouldn't have to look at Colin's wide, hurt eyes.

"I still need some time," she mumbled to the piano. "The moment has to be just right, okay? Maybe if we could be alone."

"I'm leaving for Pratt orientation in a week." The frustration in his voice was palpable. "Anyway, we're alone right now."

Hannah turned around. "No, I mean like really alone. Not here at your parents' house. Not in your car. I feel like every time we turn around, someone's"—a car door slammed outside—"interrupting," she finished.

Hannah saw Colin's jaw clench. "Damn it. I thought they'd be home later." They heard the front door open.

"It was a stupid thing to say, Carl." Colin's mother's voice cut into the quiet like a rasp.

"Don't talk to me like that, Brenda." His father's words were slightly slurred. There was a clank and then a muffled exclamation. "Who put that chair there?"

"That chair has always been there, Carl." Hannah heard the creak of the coat closet door. "Honestly, I was embarrassed—"

"Excuse me!" Colin's dad roared thickly. "I don't need you to play cop with me."

Colin stood up and grabbed Hannah's hand. "The fun never ends." He didn't look at her. "Come on, let's go out."

They stood up, but two forms suddenly blocked the light in the doorway. Hannah's heart sank, and she felt Colin stiffen beside her. Not fast enough this time.

"Oh, Colin." His mother's refined voice was higher than usual, as if she'd been tilted off balance. She gave a little laugh and smoothed her blond bob. "I didn't realize you were here. Hello, Hannah." Colin's silver-haired father stood beside her, swaying slightly on his feet, breathing alcohol fumes into the room.

"We were just leaving," Colin said roughly.

"Oh, Colin, we saw Mary Turner tonight," his mother called to their backs as they headed up the stairs. "She was asking about your photos and—"

Colin tugged Hannah down the hallway. He opened the door to the attic and closed it with a bang, cutting off his mother's plaintive strains from the floor below.

Hannah faced her boyfriend. He stood with his eyes closed and his fingertips pressed to his temples, as if to erase the scene from his brain. Hannah leaned against the wall and folded her arms. It was always best not to talk to him right away after an encounter with his parents.

Finally he lowered his hands and opened his eyes. They watched each other for a second, and then Hannah started.

"I don't know why you're so mean to them." She kept her voice neutral. "They don't seem that bad—"

"That bad!" Colin almost exploded. "The drinking, they're out all the time, and then when they do come home, it's 'Oh, Colin, how was your day? How are you? Let's talk,' like they have any idea what's going on in my life at all. But I can tell all they want to do is get away from me. They can't stand to be in the same room with me." He sank down slowly on the attic steps and leaned his head against the faded wallpaper. A pattern of green lattices hung in strips, revealing a blue and white striped paper beneath.

Hannah sat on the step beside Colin and took his hands. She peered into his face insistently until he met her gaze. "You know this is really strange, what you're saying, right? Parents don't just hate their own kids for no reason. And it's not like you're a bad person. You're so good and sweet."

Colin stared at their joined hands. His face was a mask of sadness, but the lines of anger had softened. "You don't understand. It's been like this forever—well, ever since Jack died."

Hannah bit her lip. He hardly ever mentioned his brother.

Colin rose abruptly and turned around. "Whatever. I don't want to talk about my parents anymore. Come on. I was going to show you this tomorrow, but it'll be even better at night. Do you have your camera?"

Hannah nodded and patted her big bag. "Yeah. It's so heavy to drag around, but I'm doing what you told me."

"Right. The best photos happen when you're not even looking for them."

"I know, I know!" Hannah rolled her eyes mockingly. "I'm just a beginner, okay, Great Expert?"

"Okay." His face was alight now. "Let's go."

"You're going to show me something in your attic?"

He flashed her a blinding smile. "Just wait."

Hannah raised her eyebrows but followed him upstairs anyway, the scarred wooden steps creaking under their feet.

The big attic loomed as they neared the top. There was a wide-open space in the middle, with a few bare bulbs hanging from the ceiling, throwing concentrated spots of light on the floor. Dust-cloth draped furniture sat like monoliths in the corners. Off to the sides, several doorways led to smaller rooms.

Hannah edged past an old mattress propped against one wall. Pieces of chipped paint gritted under her feet. She followed Colin into a room on the right. The doorway was smaller than the others and oddly askew. Hannah had to duck her head to avoid smacking it on the frame.

The room was piled with junk. Boxes of vinyl records were shoved against one wall, which sloped toward the eaves. Pieces of an iron bedstead were stacked against another. Several old footlocker trunks were lined up near a smeary window, under which dead moths were heavily sprinkled. The room had that hot, combustible smell of old paper and rotting plaster.

Hannah walked over to a tiny closet door. "What's in here?" she asked, putting her hand on the worn metal knob.

Colin didn't hear her. He was standing near the window, peering through the viewfinder, leather camera strap around his neck. The strap had been his grandfather's, he'd told Hannah once. He showed her the monogram, LSB, on the frayed leather. His grandfather had given it to Colin on his tenth birthday, just two weeks before he died.

"Colin? What's in this closet?" Hannah repeated, louder.

"Elves," he said, without looking up.

"Ha-ha," Hannah said automatically, but as she swung open the door, she half expected to see someone small crouching inside. Nothing though. Just strips of peeling wallpaper lying on the floor.

"So what did you want to show me up here?" she asked, closing the little closet door. "Other than elves."

Colin pulled his face away from the viewfinder and beckoned her over. "Come see."

Hannah crossed the room and looked through the window. "Oh, nice," she breathed.

The entire city was spread before them, twinkling between the black bulks of the hills. But the old glass of the window was warped, so the city lights appeared to be rolling like waves across the landscape. Hannah looked away. It made her dizzy to look through the glass—like wearing someone else's eyeglasses. She glanced over at Colin, who was grinning proudly.

"Pretty cool, huh?" He raised his camera to the window and clicked off a shot. "I noticed it the other day when I was looking through my dad's old vinyl. But I waited to take pictures until you could see it."

"Pretty cool," Hannah agreed. She raised her Pentax to her face. But she couldn't get a clear view. She kept focusing and refocusing, but still, she could tell the shots were going to come out blurry. Something about the trick of the window glass. Finally she lowered her camera. "I can't get it. The glass is too messed up. You take some for us."

"The glass is exactly what makes the effect so cool." Colin was already clicking away. Hannah let her camera drop on the strap around her neck. She wandered around the crowded room, avoiding the creepy little closet door. The air was still and unmoving. She could feel a bead of sweat start at her forehead and trickle down the side of her face.

She brushed her fingers across the tops of some medical

textbooks stacked in a box. Her fingers left clear trails in the dust. She paused at a long spotted mirror and took a shot of her own reflection. A dented olive-green file cabinet stood next to the mirror. Hannah bent down and peered at the label on the top drawer. FAMILY, it said in black ink. The drawer opened with a screech when she tugged it.

The inside was crammed with old papers and files. Hannah glanced over her shoulder at Colin. He was in full photographer mode—down on his knees now and completely absorbed in the window. Quietly she lifted her camera from around her neck and laid it on top of the cabinet. She pulled the first file from the drawer. The manila folder was soft with use, the edges fuzzy. Hannah leafed through the yellowing papers idly. Bank statements, a couple of expired passports showing Colin's parents at much younger ages. His brother Jack's old elementary school report cards. Hannah pulled out a large stained piece of paper folded in half. A photograph that was tucked inside slid out and tumbled to the floor.

"Oops." Hannah knelt to pick it up as Colin looked over at her.

"What are you doing?" He sounded vaguely annoyed, probably because she wasn't as into the window photos as he was.

"Nothing. Just poking around." She glanced at the picture—an old black and white shot, the kind with a deckled border around the edge. It showed a house perched at the edge of a lake, surrounded by pine trees. One of those big old places with a wraparound porch and a million windows. Her eyes wandered over the gabled eaves and the big bay windows. The porch was covered with elaborate curlicues. A flagstone path led up to the door, and there were pinewoods on either side. She could make out rocking chairs and a swing on the porch. At the edge of the water, there was a pale smear that Hannah guessed was a small beach. She could make out a rowboat pulled up on the sand. "Colin, where is this place? It's gorgeous." She extended the picture out to him.

He glanced at it briefly. "Was it in that file? That's nothing. It's an old vacation house my family has. We used to go up there in the summers." He turned back to the window. "Honestly, I barely remember the place." He was peering through his camera again. "All I remember is that it was ugly and boring. I hated going up there. It's probably rotting now." He focused and pressed the shutter. "I'm getting some great shots here. You don't know what you're missing."

"That's good," Hannah said absently. She unfolded the piece of paper the photo had fallen out of. It was a rough hand-drawn map. She traced her finger along a network of labeled roads. Little triangles on the sides indicated woods. Her finger with its chewed nail followed one thin line up to the top of the map where an *X* was labeled PINE HOUSE in shaky script. The place even had a name, like something in a book. A circle just beyond the *X* was labeled LAKE. Hannah flipped the map over. "1915" was inscribed on the back in the same writing. Jesus, this thing was about a century old.

She picked up the photo again. But before she could examine

it more closely, Colin turned from the window. "I think I've got everything here," he said. He looked at her hand. "Those things have probably been in that cabinet for ten years." He walked past her toward the door.

The map felt heavy in her hands. Hannah's fingers itched to lay it out once more. But Colin was already turning out the lights in the main room. Quickly she folded the picture into the map again, shoved the file back in the drawer, and hurried toward the stairs. She didn't want to be left alone in the dark.

CHAPTER 2

That night, Hannah dreamed of Pine House.

She was walking up a path toward the front door. On either side, the trees bent their whispering branches toward her, filling the air with their aromatic scent. The house sat in front of her, as if it had been waiting. She crossed the porch and touched the smooth wood of the front door. It swung open, leaving her standing in the center of a vast, airy living room. Huge windows were flung open and the fresh wind blew past her cheeks. Outside, little white-topped waves ran across the sparkling green lake like frosting. Hannah could feel the house embracing her. She dropped down in an armchair and closed her eyes. The sun was so bright on her face. . . .

Hannah opened her eyes. Her room was full of light and for a moment, she lay still, her flowered comforter still drawn up around her chin. Then she rubbed her feet together and twitched the sheet a little higher. The bed was exquisitely comfortable. She burrowed her head into her pillow just as she saw the clock alarm—8:30 a.m.

Hannah jerked upright. Damn it! She was supposed to get David ready for camp and his bus came at 8:45. And she had to work today. Hannah threw back the covers and pulled on a pair of gym shorts in one motion. She zipped a sweatshirt over her tank top, swiping her hair out of her eyes. "David, get up!" she yelled in the general direction of his room as she thundered down the stairs.

In the cluttered kitchen, Hannah found last night's dishes still in the sink and a note taped to the table.

> Han—be sure to pack David a water bottle
> in his lunch and empty the dishwasher. I'm
> closing tonight, so won't be home until 10.
> Love, Mom.

Hannah crumpled the note and pitched it at the overflowing trash can. She sloshed some milk into a glass and set it on the table just as her little brother came into the room. His eyes were only partially open and his glasses were crooked on his face. All of his hair was sticking up at the back.

"I don't want to go to camp." He slumped in a chair and stared at the milk in front of him. His T-shirt was on inside out.

"Well, I don't want to work at that stupid hospital today, but we all have to do things we don't want to do." Hannah slapped some peanut butter and strawberry jam on two slices of wheat bread and stuck it in a bag, along with the requested water bottle.

"That's different. You get to work with Laurie. I don't have *any* friends at camp."

"Just because I'm working with my friend doesn't mean it's not work." Hannah opened the fridge and peered into its depths and then added a cheese stick and an apple to the bag. "Anyway, Mom said she doesn't want you sitting around the house all summer playing Xbox."

David stared into his lunch bag. "You forgot cookies."

Hannah exhaled through her nose. "You can get them. Two Oreos, that's it." She heard the rumble of a diesel engine outside and the hydraulic wheeze of bus doors. She grabbed David by the back of his shirt and pushed him toward the door. "Go! You're going to miss it." He broke into a trot. "And fix your shirt—it's inside out!" she yelled after him. The door banged shut. The bus roared away and silence descended.

Hannah sighed. She turned to the dishwasher, lifting out the mismatched plates and bowls and stacking them on the stained Formica countertop. As her hands moved automatically, her mind went back to last night in the den with Colin. If only she could just say she loved him! He seemed so sure of himself. Graduation night two months ago, sitting in his car outside her house, he'd taken both of her hands in his and just . . . said it. His eyes had seemed so intense in the dark car, with the streetlight shining in through the windshield. Hannah could hear every rustle of their clothing, every shift of their bodies on the seat as he'd leaned over to press a long kiss on her lips.

But when it was her turn to say it, she couldn't. It was like a heavy door slamming shut inside her.

I want to, Hannah thought now, squeezing a mug in her

fingers. *I want to so badly.* She leaned on the edge of the counter for a second, tears rising in the back of her nose. Colin was so sweet, so unexpected. Even now, she couldn't believe he actually loved her—*her*! Serious, studious, responsible, boring Hannah.

But it felt like such a huge thing, telling someone you loved him like that. It had to be right. She had to be sure. She lifted a stack of plates from the dishwasher. Maybe if they had some real time alone, like she'd told Colin last night. Then she could say it.

She laid the plates carefully in the cupboard and her hand froze. Images from her dream came flooding back into her head. The open, empty room looking out onto the lake itself. The heavy pine trees rustling. Then, in her mind's eye, she saw Colin lying beside her in a hammock, the breeze blowing on their faces as they kissed.

The house—they could run away together, go up to the house. That's where they could be alone. Oh my God! She stood perfectly still, her eyes wide as the ideas ran through her mind. They could go as their last fling before he left for Pratt—if they left tomorrow, they'd have the whole weekend before his flight on Monday. It could be a surprise. She wouldn't tell him where they were going, just that they were running away together. Hannah bit back a squeal and stood on her tiptoes to shove the last of the mugs into the cabinet. She could go over to Colin's house. Just take a quick peek at the file with the map, to figure out how to get up there. She didn't have to work for another hour. Colin's mom and dad would both be gone, and Colin was at a meeting for his college orientation. He was going to pick her up afterward and drop her at the hospital with Laurie.

Hannah laced a pair of worn sneakers onto her bare feet. Her stomach had that quivery, half-giggly feeling, as if she were on a roller coaster slowly climbing toward the drop. Automatically, she looked in the hall mirror and tucked a few stray strands of hair into her ponytail. Her face stared back at her, the green eyes wide-open with excitement. A spot of red burned high on each cheekbone.

Outside, the day hung hot and humid. The maple trees lining the sidewalk brushed their leaves against Hannah's face, exhaling green, moist air. It was a fast walk to Colin's—past the elementary school, then across Springfield Pike, and then up the hill two blocks. Within ten minutes, she could see the cream clapboard and slate roof at the end of the street.

Hannah's palms grew sweaty as she approached the house. No cars in the driveway, window blinds lowered. *Okay, so far so good.* Her feet sounded unnaturally loud as she mounted the porch steps. *Calm down, it's not like you're breaking and entering.* Her tongue glued to the roof of her mouth, she pressed the doorbell and listened to the familiar chimes. No answer. *Maybe someone just didn't hear it, like last night.* Hannah pictured Colin's mother's surprised face when she saw her son's girlfriend breaking into their house. The urge to run away welled up in her stomach, but she had to get the map. The idea of escaping with Colin was too tempting, like a bag of candy held in front of her face.

Hannah crossed the porch, and as casually as she could, extracted the key from under the pansies. She resisted the urge to look left and right. She might be feeding the Byrds' cat for all the neighbors knew.

The key chattered against the lock until Hannah controlled the shake in her hand. She pushed open the heavy door and stepped into the dim foyer. The door clicked shut behind her. "Hello?" Hannah called. The silence hung in the still air. "Anyone home?" she called again. She stepped forward and tripped. A shriek bubbled to her lips. She looked down. A pair of flip-flops sat in front of the door.

Breathing a little fast, Hannah set the sandals against the wall and moved toward the staircase, treading as if about to defuse a bomb. Upstairs, Colin's parents' room was a sea of clothes and tumbled bedcovers. Colin's door was tightly shut. Hannah paused. "Hello?" she said softly. She tapped the door with her fingers, and then with one swift movement, twisted the knob.

The room was empty—just his narrow bed, made up with military neatness, and his cameras on the desk. Hannah withdrew, her face flaming, and continued down the hall.

The attic stairs creaked under her feet. The rooms at the top looked different during the day with the sunlight filtering through the dusty windows. Every scar and hole in the walls was visible. Hannah crossed to the file cabinet, keeping her eyes straight ahead, and tugged open the top drawer.

The file was right where she'd left it. Hannah felt her pulse speed up at the sight of it. She pulled it out and went down on her knees in front of the cabinet. Slowly, she opened the folder. The map was lying on top, the outline of the photo visible beneath it.

She spread the map out on the floor and flattened the creases, only vaguely aware that grit from the floor was pressing into her knees. A trickle of sweat ran down her forehead. She swiped it away impatiently and traced her finger along the map's spidery black lines. It shouldn't be too hard to find their way up there. Hannah picked up the photo from yesterday and brought it close to her eyes, but the light was dim. She gathered the map into the file and carried it across the room to the window with the trick glass. She held the picture up to the window. The dusty sunlight threw the image into sharp detail. The house wasn't new in the picture, as she'd thought yesterday. Little signs of age were scattered throughout: a railing on the porch was broken off in one corner. The screen door was torn, as if someone had put his hand through it and ripped straight down. Hannah turned the photo slowly left and right. She wished she had a magnifying glass.

Then a scratching sound came from behind her. Her heart thudded and she whirled around, the photo clutched tight in her hand. Her breath shuddered in her throat. The scratching came again. All of a sudden, she knew—*knew*—someone was hiding in the little closet across the room. She stared at the dirty little white door. A minute ticked by.

Outside, a police siren wailed up the street. Hannah jumped as if she'd been shaken. She ran from the room, clutching the file to her chest, and clattered down the stairs, leaving the heavy stillness of the attic behind her.

Her feet flew across the upstairs hallway, but a faint glassy *chink* from the floor below brought her up short. She froze, the file squeezed in her hand, her heart thudding. Someone *was* home. The cleaning lady? Some unseen repairman? Hannah slid her feet silently across the carpet toward the front stairs. Another *chink*. This time she could place the noise—an ice cube against the side of a glass. Probably not a repairman. It was coming from the kitchen, at the rear of the house. If she could just get down the stairs undetected, she could still slip out the front door without whomever it was seeing her.

Hannah crept silently down the top flight to the landing and then to the bottom flight. Her hand, greasy with sweat, slid along the banister as if oiled. She only faintly registered that her breath was coming in short, quick puffs.

She reached the bottom of the stairs and crossed quickly to the door. Her hand was on the knob when someone behind her said, "Hello, Hannah."

Hannah whirled around. Mrs. Byrd stood in the doorway from the living room, her hair mussed, and a glass in her hand, mostly full of a clear liquid. She wore a charcoal gray suit, as if she'd been going to work, but the jacket was unbuttoned and her silk blouse hung untucked. Her feet were bare.

Hannah shoved the file behind her back, aware of how guilty she must look. But Mrs. Byrd didn't seem to notice, nor did she ask what Hannah was doing creeping around the house in the middle of the day. She focused somewhere over Hannah's shoulder. "How are you, dear? Come talk to me a bit. Would you like some iced tea?" Without waiting for an answer, she turned and walked back through the living room, disappearing through the opposite doorway leading to the kitchen.

For a moment, Hannah didn't move from her position by the door. Then she bent and carefully slid the file under an oriental-patterned throw rug at her feet before following Mrs. Byrd.

Colin's mother sat at the kitchen table, a bottle of vodka beside her, along with a jar of olives. She didn't look up at Hannah standing uneasily in the doorway and instead, stared ahead of her at the massive stainless-steel refrigerator, moodily sipping from her glass.

The kitchen clock ticked off a minute, then another. Hannah waited. She wondered how long it would be before Mrs. Byrd asked her why she was sneaking around in the house. Finally she couldn't stand the silence any longer. She cleared her throat. "Um, I was just picking up Colin's camera for him—"

"The camera!" Mrs. Byrd's voice was harsh. "Spends more time hiding behind it than talking to his own mother."

Hannah stepped back warily. Mrs. Byrd still didn't look at her. Hannah wondered if she even realized whom she was talking to.

"Cold. He's a cold, cold boy," Colin's mother said to the refrigerator. Her words were slurred slightly. "We've always tried to protect him, you know that? It's been so hard. Jack's been gone seven years. Such a bad world. Tried to protect him, and this is how he repays us." She gulped at her glass.

Hannah's hand trembled on the door frame. Mrs. Byrd was drunk, that was obvious. Maybe Hannah could just slip away. Mrs.

Byrd might not even notice. Hannah quietly eased toward the door.

Mrs. Byrd's stalk-like neck swung around abruptly. She focused on Hannah. "You're a good girl, though." Her lips stretched back over her teeth. "Good for him. You make him happy, even I can see that. Even his crazy drunk of a mother can see that." Her barked laughter lingered in the air like smoke. She fell silent, staring back into the oily depths of her glass.

Hannah took one step backward, then another. She had to get out of here. Her stomach felt sick and her armpits were clammy and damp. "Um, yeah, well, thanks, Mrs. Byrd," she babbled. "I'm late so—" She spun around and ran through the living room and into the foyer, pausing only to grab the file from under the rug. She yanked open the front door and shoved the key back under the pansies before fleeing.

A block away, she slowed to a fast walk. The street seemed unusually bright and busy after the grim chill of Colin's kitchen. The sunlight danced on the sidewalk and finches flitted from branch to branch overhead.

What if Colin's mother had seen the file? Hannah thought suddenly, pressing her hand over her heart and feeling the thumps. *She hadn't. She was totally out of it.* There was some weird tension between Colin and his parents, for sure. Colin was really upset last night. Maybe this trip could be a break from his parents too. Hannah held the precious documents inside her shirt like a criminal. *Stealing, that's what you did,* a voice in her head said. *Not stealing,* she argued silently. She was just borrowing. Borrowing something no one wanted—except her.

CHAPTER 3

Safe back in her own bedroom, Hannah closed the door behind her and rested against it for a second, trying to slow her panting. The file burned against her chest. She moved it out from under her shirt and laid it carefully in her desk drawer, gazing at it before sliding the drawer shut. A smile curled the edges of her mouth. It would be like living together—even sleeping in the same bed all night. She and Colin hadn't actually had sex—she wanted to wait until college and Colin had always been okay with that. But this would be much better than making out in his room and then driving herself home with her hair all messed up and her lips chafed. At the lake house, she wouldn't have to leave.

Hannah barely had time to splash some water on her face and exchange her shorts for jeans before Colin's horn sounded outside. She ran downstairs and grabbed her bag before climbing into the familiar front seat of his pickup.

"Morning." Colin smiled at her from behind his aviator

sunglasses. He pulled her toward him as she banged the door shut, and kissed her on the lips. His eyebrows jumped. "What have you been doing?" he asked.

She could feel the blood drain from her face. "Nothing. Why?" She glanced down at herself. Could he tell? Some stray dust smear? She noticed deep pink welts on her knees from kneeling on the gritty attic floor. Quietly, she rested her hands over them.

Colin craned his neck to reverse down the driveway, his arm along the back of the seat. "You're all sweaty. Did you go running or something?"

Hannah exhaled and willed the blood to stop pounding in her ears. "Oh. Yeah. Just a couple miles. Sorry—I didn't have time for a shower. Gross, right?" She could taste the lie on her lips along with the salty sweat.

Colin grinned as he accelerated down the street. "I like you all dirty." He leaned over and mock-bit her on the neck.

Hannah squealed automatically and pushed him away. "Watch out! Don't crash us on my first day of work." The playful words sounded hollow. She thought of Colin's empty bedroom. Her hand on the door of the attic only an hour ago. She'd stolen from his house, and he had no idea. She'd never hidden anything from him before.

Colin turned onto a busy boulevard thick with early morning traffic. He accelerated past a tire shop and a real-estate office and negotiated the truck around a road crew digging something up in the middle of the street.

"Thanks for driving me, by the way," Hannah said. "I would have been okay with the bus."

"I know," Colin said a little too quickly.

There was a tiny, faintly awkward pause as Hannah looked out the window and Colin focused on the road. They usually didn't run into the whole money thing too often but Hannah still felt a little pang of embarrassment whenever it came up. And for some reason she couldn't put her finger on, the fact that Colin always seemed embarrassed too made it worse.

"Hey!" Colin braked suddenly and turned the car into a tiny parking lot squeezed between a dry cleaners and the back of an elementary school. A wooden sign above a sagging brick building read FRIDA'S in curling script letters. "Let's get some breakfast."

"I'm totally late already!"

Colin glanced at the dashboard clock. "You don't have to be there until ten, right? So, we have twelve minutes. Besides, we have to celebrate your first day at work."

Hannah grinned. "Celebrate my first day hauling around boxes with Laurie?" She could already smell the delicious scent of burnt sugar in the air when she opened the car door.

"Yeah." Colin looped his arm around her neck and matched his strides to hers as they walked toward the entrance. "Or celebrate the fact that I'm about to eat six doughnuts in a row."

"Remember when we used to come here all the time last fall?" Hannah pushed the door open. The burnt-sugar scent was even stronger inside the warm, high-ceilinged room. Commuters stood crowding the counter, jockeying for prime positions to grab raspberry-cheese cups and lattes. Students with messenger bags strapped to their chests and headphones snaking from their ears, hustled past them out the door, clutching the familiar white, waxy bags already spotted with translucent grease.

"Grab a seat." Colin nudged her toward the rickety vintage tables against one wall. "I'll get the stuff."

"Caramel doughnut and mint tea!" Hannah called as she perched on a leather-topped metal chair. Pushing aside someone else's *New York Times*, she propped her head on her fist and watched Colin navigate his way to the front of the crowd. She thought of how awkward they were when they'd first started coming here, sitting in the big armchairs in the corner, trying to think of things to say as they turned the white mugs around and around in their hands. Eating éclairs and trying to keep the chocolate off her teeth. How she couldn't believe that she, *Hannah*, was actually sitting with a guy—and not a nerdy guy either, but blond-god Colin.

She smiled at Colin as he returned, balancing two plates and a tea mug. "Can you believe we've been together almost a year?" she asked as he sat down opposite her. She blew on her tea, the grassy mint fragrance bathing her face.

Colin bit off half a glazed doughnut. "No." His cheeks were distended as he chewed. "It's weird to think about it like that."

"There'll be tons of cute, arty chicks at Pratt. They're probably all photographers too." Hannah eyed him and nibbled the sticky top of her caramel doughnut. Joni Mitchell started up on the music system overhead.

"So?" He shoved the rest of the doughnut in his mouth and spoke with difficulty. "I don't want a cute, arty chick. I want you."

"Nerd-queen and boy-god. Least likely couple." She sipped her tea.

"We weren't 'least likely.' That was Tabitha and Jon." He wiped his mouth with a napkin, missing a sprinkling of dough-nut sugar.

Hannah leaned over and brushed her fingers over his cheek. "You know what I mean. You're the first guy who treated me like I was visible at all."

"Han, I could see you right away. The minute I met you." He squeezed her hand back and stood up, pointing at her barely-touched doughnut. "You want me to get you a bag? We should go. You'll be late and then Laurie will have a heart attack and you won't have a summer job anymore."

Hannah slid her arm around his waist and laid her head on his shoulder as they walked back to the car. Colin started the engine and pulled back onto the boulevard.

"Okay, so it's up Vine Street, right?" He peered through the windshield at the street signs.

"Yeah, Bethesda North. Past Montgomery, then left on Poage Farm Road," she told him.

They drove for a moment in silence. Then Colin took a deep breath. "Listen, I'm sorry about last night," he said abruptly.

"What?"

He threw her a glance. "You know, about the whole, um, discussion in the den. It was just that after graduation, you said you just needed more time. So I thought maybe it had been long enough." He reached over and squeezed her hand. She clung tightly to his. "I'm sorry I was so intense."

"Thanks." She bit her lip as guilt started to weigh her down again. He was being so sweet, so open and honest, and she was the one hiding something. She stared down at their intertwined hands. His long fingers, the nails neatly filed against her gnawed ones. "Colin?"

"What?" He was trying to negotiate a busy left turn.

She fidgeted in the seat, pressing the window button up and down. "Do you think . . . there's ever a good reason to do something, um, wrong?" She choked a little on the last word.

He threw her a quizzical look. "I don't know. You mean like questioning authority?"

"Sort of." A little knot of tension started at the back of her neck as she thought of this morning. She'd actually forgotten it for a few minutes while they were at Frida's. "Like if you knew that doing something wrong would actually turn out right in the end."

Colin shrugged and turned into the hospital parking lot. "Sure, I guess that would be okay." He faced her. "Hannah, is there something you want to tell me?" he asked seriously.

She stared at him, frozen, before she saw the playful smile twisting his mouth. He poked her in the thigh and laughed. "Got you! You looked so guilty just then. What have you been doing, stealing cars again?"

Hannah giggled in spite of herself, his easy voice steadying her like always. "You're hilarious. David was just asking me about . . . civil rights this morning. That's all." She hoisted her bag onto her shoulder and leaned across the seat to peck him on the cheek. "Thanks for the ride."

She watched as the black truck roared out of the parking lot, and then turned toward the gleaming glass and metal hospital entrance. The automatic doors opened and closed constantly as a steady stream of doctors in scrubs, visitors bearing gifts, and patients in wheelchairs flowed in and out. Hannah turned right, skirting an elderly man manipulating a walker up the curb. Instead of going into the spacious, gleaming lobby, she followed the perimeter of the building to the back as her friend Laurie had instructed her. Hannah consulted a piece of paper in her hand and then squinted across the parking lot at several squat concrete buildings crouched next to a fence.

Laurie's rickety Corolla was parked in front of a partly chocked open door. As Hannah crossed over to it, her friend emerged from the doorway, hair in a business-like ponytail, holding a big box. "It's ten sixteen," she called before setting the box on the ground. "I wanted to start right at ten."

"Hi to you too." Hannah gave her friend a hug. "Relax, would you? Aren't we working by ourselves?" Laurie was the only person Hannah knew who was more uptight than herself. She followed her friend into the building. It was a little dark room, with one small window covered in wire mesh. The place was filled with boxes stacked almost to the ceiling. Hannah gazed at the scene, her hands on her hips. "This is what we're doing?" she said.

Laurie's father owned a business-relocation service, and Laurie worked for him in the summer. Companies would hire them when they were moving offices, and they'd make sure all their stuff got out of the old place and into the new place safely. Hannah had agreed immediately when Laurie's dad had offered her a summer job. Mom was counting on her to make some extra cash. But now she wondered if she should have thought it through a bit more.

"Yeah," Laurie answered, surveying the mess with a practiced eye. She'd been working for her dad since she was old enough to walk. "The hospital hasn't used these buildings for years. They're going to raze them, but we have to get all of this stuff from here to there." She pointed to an identical room next door.

"What?" Hannah raised her eyebrows. "Why are we moving this stuff twenty feet to exactly the same room?"

Laurie shrugged. "That's just what the guy said." She seemed unfazed.

Hannah felt her shoulders sag as she stared at the dirty little room. The days of summer seemed to stretch out in front of her like miles on a flat asphalt road. She bent down and grasped a box at her feet.

For a long time, she and Laurie lifted, carried, and stacked in silence. Hannah's forearms and chest quickly became powdered with moldy black dust. Her leg muscles burned from the unaccustomed exertion. The thought of the photo sitting under her mattress itched like a maddening tickle. She hoisted another box and imagined the sound of the lake lapping at the shore. Laurie

30

worked like an automaton beside her, and Hannah could sense she didn't want talking to slow them down.

Finally the last box was transferred, and the little room was empty except for a coating of the black dust everywhere. Now the other room looked just like the first. Hannah pulled her Nalgene from her bag and stepped outside. The dry brown grass next to the parking lot looked like an oasis. She sank down cross-legged, took a long swig of water, and then offered it to Laurie, who sat down beside her.

Laurie emptied half the bottle in one gulp. "It's hot in there," she said, wiping her forehead with the hem of her T-shirt.

Hannah snorted. "That's a slight understatement." She leaned back, resting her hands on the prickly grass and squinting against the glare of the sunshine. "So, what's the next job?"

Laurie wrinkled her forehead, thinking. "Oh, it's a big one. Saturday. Moving the chemistry library at the university to their new building. We'll have some guys to help us with that one."

Hannah nodded. She pictured an endless linoleum hallway, lined front to back with taped-up boxes. "Laurie, do you ever want to escape somewhere?" The words popped out of her mouth as if someone else were speaking.

Laurie blinked. "Well, yeah, I guess," she said slowly. She indicated the little building behind them. "But obviously, I can't. I have to work. My dad's counting on me."

Hannah slowly screwed the top on the water bottle and balanced it between her feet. "But can't you just tell him you don't want to for awhile?"

"Sure." Laurie barked a laugh. "And then he'd disown me, but that's no problem. Look, Han, there's no use living in fantasyland. You can't just leave." She leveled her friend with a keen stare. "Is this about Colin?"

Hannah tried to ignore the flush that rose automatically up her neck. "Why?" She raked the grass with her fingers nonchalantly.

"Oh, no reason." Laurie lay down flat and crooked her arm over her eyes. "It's just that this girl I know has this boyfriend who's leaving for New York in, oh I don't know, a few days, and they've been having this issue with these three little, teeny words, and all of a sudden out of nowhere, she starts talking about escaping, so no—no reason at all."

"Laurie, listen." Hannah's hands tightened convulsively on the grass next to her. A sense of urgency swept over her. "I just want to get away with him, escape, before he goes off to Pratt next week. It'll be like the big finale of our year together. And maybe I can say it then."

Laurie sighed and sat up. "You know, you'd have a much easier time if you just *lied* about it, Han," she said dryly. "You could just say it even if it's not one hundred percent true. What if it's eighty percent true? Would that be okay?"

Hannah shook her head emphatically. "No. This is huge! I have to be completely sure the first time I say it."

Laurie smiled at her friend, the habitually tight lines in her face relaxing. "You're so earnest. But you're right—it's important. You should mean it completely." She climbed to her feet, dusting off her rear with both hands. "Come on. There's a second room to move."

Hannah followed slowly. A fly dive-bombed her ear, and she swatted at it impatiently. "You *can* just leave, you know," she said, but too quietly for Laurie to hear.

CHAPTER 4

When Hannah came downstairs the next morning, Mom was hunched over the kitchen table. A mug of coffee sat in front of her, along with the remains of a piece of toast. She glanced at the kitchen clock. "Isn't six a little early for you, Han?" she asked. She was already wearing her bright purple bookstore shirt. Her thin brown hair, streaked with gray, was drawn into a ponytail and faint webs of wrinkles fanned out around her faded blue eyes.

Hannah perched at the edge of a chair. Today was the day. She had the escape plan firmly in her mind. Mom was the most important hurdle. If she could just get her to agree to the trip, she could leave with Colin when he picked her up for work this morning. Except they wouldn't be going to work. They'd be going away. Hannah's her stomach gave a little jump at the thought.

"You want a piece of toast, honey?" Mom asked.

Hannah shook her head. "I'm not hungry."

"Okay." Mom was focusing on a note in front of her. "Listen,

I need you to go to the store today, okay? I'm making you a list. Just get some lunch things . . ." She scribbled with a chewed Bic.

Hannah clasped her hands on the table in front of her. "Mom, something's come up."

"Hmm?" Now her mother was rummaging through her worn leather handbag. "I think I have a coupon here for yogurt."

"Mom." Hannah raised her voice a little. "Listen. Stop with the list. Laurie wants me to do an out-of-town job with her. Starting this afternoon. It's a last minute thing." She choked a little on the lie but managed to get it out.

"What?" Mom looked up, her face creased. "An out-of-town job? Hannah, you can't. I need you here. There's David, and the house. They scheduled me for double shifts through the weekend." She shook her head and continued her search for the coupon. "Tell Laurie's dad you can't, okay? I don't know what he's thinking, that you could just leave like that. . . . Ah!" She held up a wrinkled scrap of paper. "Found it."

The beep of a car horn sounded outside. Mom jumped up. "That's the carpool. Listen, make sure David has something green with his dinner, okay?" She pushed back her chair and picked up her bag.

"Mom," Hannah said desperately. "He's going to pay me triple time." She resisted the urge to clutch at her mother's sleeve. "Mrs. Robinson can watch David while you're at work. She owes us for dog sitting anyway. And it's just for a couple of days." She gripped the edge of the table, feeling the scratchy sawdust underside on her fingertips.

Mom paused. "Triple time? That's very generous of him."

"Yeah." Hannah nodded her head like a marionette. "And travel expenses, too. Think of how the extra money would come in handy. And I'll have my cell the whole time." She could feel the lies piling up, like a big bundle she had to carry, but she couldn't stop the words from spilling out.

Another beep outside, this one longer. Mom looked at the clock. "Oh God, I'm really late." She slung her purse over her shoulder. "Look, Han, let's talk about it tonight when I get home, okay?"

"Mom! He wants to leave this afternoon." Hannah clasped her hands in front of her chest. "I'll get David to Mrs. Robinson's as soon as he wakes up. She's right next door. He can get the camp bus from there." A frantic feeling welled up in her chest. Mom had to agree. She had to. Hannah would run away if she didn't. She'd just leave—take off. She followed her mother into the front hall. "Please!"

Mom had her hand on the doorknob. "All right. All right!" she said. "But I don't like the idea of you careening around God knows where. Write down where you'll be and Laurie's dad's cell, too." Hannah flew forward and pecked Mom on her thin cheek.

Mom hugged her and Hannah was enveloped in her familiar cinnamon scent. Then she was gone, out the door, and climbing into the rust-eaten blue sedan chugging in the driveway.

"Yes!" Hannah wilted against the wall, all the intensity draining away. She closed her eyes. She saw her and Colin sitting in the porch swing at Pine House. The lake made little lapping sounds on the beach. Colin smiled at her. His eyes perfectly matched the blue of the sky behind his head. He leaned over to kiss her—

"Hannah?" David stood sleep-rumpled on the stairs. He rubbed a fist over his eye. "You woke me up."

"I'm sorry."

He looked very vulnerable in his limp football pajamas, with his hair sticking up in whorls. Hannah turned abruptly and walked toward the kitchen.

"Dave, I'm going to be leaving for a little while." She busied herself extracting the frying pan from the crowded cupboard.

"What? Where're you going?"

Hannah cracked an egg into a glass. "To a job with Laurie out of town. It's just for the weekend." She kept her face turned toward the stove.

"But who's going to get me ready in the morning? And make dinner?"

Hannah faced him. He stood in the middle of the kitchen, his forehead wrinkled. His bony shoulders pushed at the soft, thin fabric of his shirt. Hannah swallowed. "Dave, it's going to be fine. Mrs. Robinson's going to watch you while Mom's gone. You can go over there after camp today. Maybe she'll let you take the dog for a walk."

David looked doubtful. Hannah gave his shoulders a squeeze. "And I'm making you French toast too."

As soon as David was done eating, Hannah steered him across the dewy grass to Mrs. Robinson's clapboard bungalow next door.

Economy-size bags of dog food were stacked on the porch three deep, as usual. Hannah rang the bell. David gazed up at her dolefully. "She's going to make me eat those old cookies again. They had mold on them last time," he whispered.

"Just say you're full from breakfast," Hannah muttered back as the door squeaked open and Mrs. Robinson peered around the edge.

"Davey!" she cried, smiling with her impossibly white teeth. She swung the door open. Her hair was newly dyed and more stridently pink than usual, Hannah noted.

"Hi, Mrs. Robinson," she said loudly. "I have to go out of town this weekend suddenly, and my mom and I were wondering if you could watch David in the morning before camp and in the afternoon. Just for a couple days."

"Of course, of course!" Mrs. Robinson already had her arm around David's shoulders and was ushering him inside. Hannah wasn't sure if she'd even heard everything she'd told her.

"I just found some cookies hiding in the cupboard, waiting for this young man to eat them," she caroled. "Have a nice time on your trip."

The storm door swung shut in Hannah's face and David cast her one last desperate glance over his shoulder before he disappeared around the corner.

Back in the house, Hannah went straight up to her room, leaving the dirty dishes on the counter. As she drew her duffel bag from the closet, the quivery feeling started in her stomach again. In the space of twenty-four hours, she had snuck into someone's house, taken something that wasn't hers, and lied to her mother. She'd never done that many bad things in her entire life before. *Am I going crazy?* And leaving David too . . . he was going to miss her. Her hands faltered a minute, buried in the ruffly folds of a sundress as she paused, staring off into space. Then she shook her head and stuffed the sundress into the bag. It was worth it. This might be her only chance to run away with a guy, ever. And not just any guy—Colin. *Oh my God, I am actually going to do this.* She threw jeans and tank tops into the bag and then folded her bikini before sticking a pair of strappy sandals and her hiking boots on top.

She giggled, a trifle hysterically. *Okay, calm down. Colin will be here any minute. Don't forget the map!* She plucked the file from its hiding place under the mattress. She couldn't leave that. They'd never find the place and wind up at Sea World instead. Actually, maybe she should Google it too, just to be safe.

Hannah pulled out her desk chair and flipped open her laptop. She poised her fingers over the keyboard, and then paused. The address. Of course, there was no address on the map. Doubtfully, Hannah typed "Pine House" into the search bar. Nothing.

She drummed her fingers on the keys, then examined the map spread out beside her. A tiny dot down from the house was labeled OXTOWN. She typed that into Google. Nothing again. The old map was going to have to be it for directions. Luckily there was a highway exit marked in pen, obviously added later on. Hannah recognized the exit. It was on the other side of the state, a good four hours drive away. Maybe once they got there, the old map would make more sense.

Hannah pushed back her chair and shut down the computer. Then she grabbed her phone from the bedside table and thumbed Laurie's number. The phone rang once, twice.

"Hi," Laurie answered. "What's up? Did you and Colin elope yet?"

"Almost!" Hannah knew she was squealing, but she couldn't help it. "Listen, I have a huge favor to ask you." Briefly she filled Laurie in on her discovery of Pine House and the plan to leave. "So, will you cover for me? Tell my mom I'm with you if she calls?" She waited breathlessly, squeezing the phone tight in one hand.

"Okay, let's see. You're ditching me on the second day of work to go off on a romantic weekend with your sexy boyfriend. I'm supposed to be thrilled about this?"

Hannah winced. "Not thrilled, just helpful. Please? I-love-you-forever-you're-my-best-friend, please?"

There was a long pause and then Laurie sighed. "Okay. But only if you promise to tell me every detail of everything that happens. Nothing left out!"

"Thank you, thank you. You're a goddess." Hannah made kissing noises at the phone.

"Damn right I am." Laurie hung up.

Hannah slid the phone into her pocket and paced around the room, chewing her cuticles and plotting her next move. She'd get Colin to take her over to his house, and she'd pack him a bag. Then she'd tell him they were going on a surprise road trip. She smiled to herself as she thought of his face when he found out they were going away together. And his parents weren't going to be a problem like Mom. They didn't say anything when he took off to go skiing in Vermont over winter break, and that was for two weeks.

Outside, Colin's truck was idling in the driveway. The day could not have been more gorgeous if Disney had designed it—azure sky complete with puffy, high white clouds. Technicolor tulips waving from the neighbors' lawns.

"Hey there." Colin's bright hair was still wet from the shower. He smelled of Irish Spring soap and fresh laundry.

Biting back a grin, she threw her duffel behind the seat and climbed in. "Hey." She kept her face turned toward the window as he started down the street. A fresh breeze blew through both open windows, ruffling her hair.

Quietly, she unzipped the canvas tote on her lap and slipped her hand inside. "Damn."

Colin glanced over with mild surprise. "What?"

"Oh, nothing." She rummaged around in the bag. "It's just that I think I left my wallet at your house when we were there the other day. And I need my license for work today." The lie came out smoothly. She was getting better at this.

"No problem." Colin signaled and turned left instead of right at the end of the street. "We'll just drop by my place and get it."

Hannah nodded and settled back in the seat.

When Colin turned into his driveway, he switched off the engine and started to follow her, but she held her hand out. "It's okay, I know exactly where it is. Be right back."

He shrugged. "Okay, I'll just wait for you." He tossed her the keys and sat back in the driver's seat, lacing his fingers behind his head.

Inside the empty house, Hannah ran up the stairs and into Colin's room. She looked around quickly. Spotting his backpack by the desk, she unzipped it and dumped out the jumble of notebooks and pens inside. She stuffed in handfuls of T-shirts, jeans, and shorts from his dresser, and then added a pair of sneakers, some socks and boxers. She grabbed his camera from its place next to his bed and crammed that in too. Zipping into the bathroom, she grabbed his razor, deodorant, and a bar of green soap from the shower. With difficulty, she tugged closed the bulging zipper, and then heaved the bag onto her back. She threw a glance out the window. The truck was in the driveway, Colin reclining in the front seat. His elbow stuck out the window. *He has no idea the best time of his life is about to start happening now,* she thought.

She flew down the stairs. In the foyer, she paused an instant, imagining Mrs. Byrd's figure in the living room doorway. Then she shuddered and ran out the front door.

Colin's brow creased when he saw the backpack. "What's going on?" he asked as she threw it next to her own and climbed in again.

Hannah inhaled. "Colin," she said. "I'm not going to work today."

His eyebrows lifted. "You're not?"

"Nope," she said. The grin she'd been suppressing since he

picked her up finally broke through. "We're going on a road trip this weekend."

"No way!" he said. "Like, right now?"

She nodded. "I thought you'd like a surprise."

"Like it!" He leaned over and planted a long kiss on her lips.

Hannah threw her arms around his neck. "This is our last fling, you know, before you leave. I thought it would be fun to run away together for a couple days." She spoke into the warm crook of his neck.

He pulled away a little so he could look down into her face. "Han, this is so awesome." His eyes were sparkling. "Totally unlike you, of course. Remember when you got all mad at me for sneaking into your room last year?"

"You freaked me out climbing up the porch like that. I thought you were an ax murderer or something."

Colin gunned the truck's engine and backed down the driveway. "So, where're we going?"

Hannah looked at him sideways. "That's a secret."

Colin laughed. "This just keeps getting better and better." He reached over and squeezed her knee, steering with the other hand. "What happened to responsible Hannah Taylor?"

Hannah bit her lip and imagined the file glowing behind her as if illuminated by an X-ray. "She took a break for a while." She leaned back. "Your parents won't care, right?"

Colin exhaled through his nose. "Forget them." Keeping one eye on the road, he speed-dialed on his cell. The corners of his lips were tight as he waited for the phone to ring. "Hi, Mom.

Listen, something's come up, okay? I'm going to take off for a couple of days." He listened to the voice on the other end and his nostrils flared. "Nothing big, okay? Trent's just going to his dad's cabin for a few days and he wants me to come, that's all. I'll be back"—he paused and eyed Hannah—"on Sunday?"

Hannah nodded. She could hear his mom's voice in little squawks over the receiver.

"Okay. Mmhmm. Yeah. Bye." He snapped the phone closed and pretended to fling it out the window. "Thank God that's over."

Hannah blew out her lips. "Was she okay with it?" she said.

Colin shrugged. "Who cares? They'll probably be relieved I'm gone. No big sullen teenage son slouching around the house." He tapped out a little rhythm on the steering wheel. "So! Which direction should I go? Or is that part a secret too?"

Hannah closed her eyes and pictured the map in her head. "Just take I-70 north. I'll tell you what to do after that."

They waded through the heavy city traffic for the next ten miles or so, and then gradually, the cars thinned along with the exits. The office parks and subdivisions were replaced by endless flat fields of corn on one side and soybeans on the other. Occasionally the monotony was relieved by a few black and white cows scattered in a field. Giant billboards advertised TRUCKERS' WORLD, GIRLS XXX, and IF JESUS CAME TODAY, WOULD YOU BE READY?

Hannah snuck a glance over at Colin, who was nodding his head along with the oldies music on the radio. He must have sensed her look because he grinned suddenly and reached over to pull her against his shoulder.

"So, you're really not telling me where we're going?" he asked.

"Nope." Hannah pressed her face against his T-shirt, feeling its moleskin softness against her cheek.

"Can I guess?"

She straightened up and grinned. "Go ahead. I'll tell you if you're right, but you'll never guess."

Colin wrinkled his forehead ostentatiously. "Alaska."

"Ha-ha."

"Greece."

"You're doing great," she told him. "Keep going."

"Thailand—no, wait, I've got it. New Zealand."

"Yes! That's it." Hannah leaned over and kissed him on the cheek. "You guessed it. We're driving this truck straight to New Zealand and never coming back."

"Now *that* sounds like a great idea." Colin glanced over, and his eyes were alight. "Running away together somewhere cool for as long as we wanted."

Hannah smiled at the thought and clasped his free hand. "Just hiking around and sleeping under the stars."

"We should do it. Instead of me going to Pratt, let's backpack around the world."

"Right!" Hannah laughed. "I'll just make sure I'm back for my mom's funeral because she'd keel over if I ever told her I was doing that."

"That's why this trip now is such a great surprise." Colin squeezed her hand. "It's like a little taste of that life."

They drove in companionable silence for a while. Hannah

idly flipped through the radio channels, eventually settling on a bluegrass station. Occasionally, Colin looked over at her with a questioning glance but she just smiled at him mysteriously.

After a couple of hours, she lifted her cramped legs up onto the dashboard and pointed her toes. She stretched her arms over her head. Colin cracked his neck from side to side. "So, mystery woman, when's the surprise up?" he asked idly, draping an arm over the back of her seat and rubbing her neck with his fingers.

Hannah glanced at him. Maybe now was the time. They were almost halfway to the highway exit. She took a deep breath and twisted around to her duffel. Straining over the center console, she managed to unzip the bag and pull out the file. She placed it carefully in her lap.

Colin glanced over and then back at the road. "What's that?"

Instead of answering, Hannah opened the file and held up the photo. She could feel a silly grin spread over her lips as she waited for his response.

Colin shot a glance at the photo. "I don't get it. That's the old picture from the attic. How'd you get that?"

"Colin." Hannah shook her head. She couldn't believe he still didn't understand. "The lake house. Pine House. We're going to Pine House. I have the map and everything, right here." She held her breath, watching his face.

"Wait," he said slowly. "This is the road trip? Going up to the old lake house?"

"Yeah."

"And that's why you told me to go this way."

46

She nodded, still smiling, but a little worm of worry began to uncurl itself in her stomach. His voice was so calm and so cold, like a stranger's. Was it the map? Was he mad she took it? Hannah felt her face flush with shame. She couldn't look at him, fixing her eyes instead on the road ahead. Silence settled heavily over the truck, a long silence, which seemed to have no end.

CHAPTER 5

After a few minutes, Colin glanced in the rearview mirror and then moved into the right lane. He pulled onto the shoulder and slowed rapidly, the rumble strip thrumming loudly under the truck's wheels. Before Hannah could fully comprehend what he was doing, he parked the car, turned off the ignition, and then sat still with his hands on the wheel.

Without the engine, the cab seemed even quieter. The silence was broken only by the regular *whoosh* of cars zooming by outside, rocking the truck a little each time. For a long time, Colin stared straight ahead. Then he said very softly, "How'd you get the photo and the map, Han?" His breath whistled as he spoke.

Just relax. He's surprised, that's all. She swallowed. "I . . . I took them." She avoided the word "stole." She hadn't really, anyway.

He nodded without changing expression. "When?" The single word floated on the air between them.

Briefly, she explained—the spare key, the attic file cabinet.

"It was all for us, Colin." She leaned over, trying to look into his eyes. "I wanted so much for us to have a place to be alone now, before you went to orientation. So we could talk about, you know, the, um, love thing."

He swung his head around, his fingers clenched tight on the steering wheel. She shrank back against the door at the sight of his eyes blazing, standing out like glowing jewels against his suddenly pale face. "I never thought you'd be the type to steal, Hannah," he said icily. "I must not know you as well as I thought. Just like you obviously don't know me if you think I'd actually want to go up to that dump. I told you I hated it—nothing's changed."

Hannah recoiled against the door as his fury filled the cab. She stared at him, unable to reconcile this blazing stranger with her gentle Colin. She felt disoriented, like someone had spun her around and shoved her off into an unknown direction. She had to get out and get some air. Hannah fumbled for the door handle and pulled it. She almost toppled from the seat as she scrambled onto the gravel shoulder.

The *swishing* of the cars shook her as she stumbled across the drainage ditch at the side of the road. A wire and post fence stretched along the shoulder. Beyond it, a cornfield rose in a wall of emerald green. High up on a rise sat a tidy ranch house with an American flag fluttering outside.

Hannah clutched at the fence. The wire was cool under her fingers. The corn leaves rustled in the wind like paper. She inhaled a long hitching breath, trying not to cry. Her stomach felt sick and her hands and feet were icy cold.

Behind her, the truck door opened and closed. A second later, Colin's hand touched her back. She didn't turn around.

She heard him swallow. "Hannah."

She stared at the corn.

"Han. I'm sorry. I totally overreacted back there."

She turned around. He stood in front of her with hunched shoulders, his hands stuffed in his pockets. He looked smaller outside of the car, shrunken somehow.

"What's the deal?" she asked. Her voice was thick with suppressed tears. "You've never been so angry before. I thought you wanted to go away with me."

Colin stared at his feet. "I do. I really do. It's just—I don't know, the place gets on my nerves, even though I hardly remember it." He looked up at her, his face pleading. "Does that sound totally crazy?"

Hannah hesitated. "Maybe it's different than you remember." She took both of his hands in hers and then dropped them in surprise. His palms were drenched.

"Are you okay?" she asked. The collar of his T-shirt was dark with sweat too. Damp patches had appeared under his arms.

Colin closed his eyes and squeezed his temples with his fingers. "Yeah, I'm okay. I just feel a little strange." He tried to smile at her, but Hannah could see that the grin wasn't real.

"Okay," she said slowly. "So . . . what do you think? Can we go up? Colin, I think we're going to have fun. It'll be like a real vacation. What do you think? Please?" She clasped her hands in front of her chest in supplication.

Colin laughed hollowly. "Okay," he said. "Anything for you."

"Thank you!" She flung her arms around his neck and was relieved to feel him hug her back.

"Hey," Colin said as they walked toward the truck. "Let me take a look at that old picture. I never really saw it when we were up in the attic." His voice sounded normal at last.

"Oh, it's so cool," she said excitedly, running ahead to get the file. She grabbed it from the truck seat, first putting the map on the dashboard, and then handed the file to Colin, who stood on the shoulder, waiting.

He turned away from the road and opened the folder. "Careful," Hannah said. "Don't let it blow away." She picked up the photo. "Look, you can see the lake." She smiled, watching for the moment the creases smoothed from his brow.

He held the photo up in front of him, examining it in the sunlight, while the harsh highway wind pulled at their hair and the vague smell of cow manure drifted from the pasture, mixing with the diesel exhaust from the semis that rumbled past.

At last Colin snapped the file closed. "Cool. Hey, let's go, right? It's getting late. How much farther do we have?"

"Not too far, I think." Hannah walked ahead of him to the truck and climbed in, grabbing the map to check the name of the exit again. Colin banged the driver's door shut. He started the engine and with a quick glance in his side mirror, pulled out on the road, pressing the accelerator to the floor. The truck swung onto the highway, fishtailing slightly.

Hannah opened her mouth to say something about the speed

when she realized what was missing. She looked in her own side mirror. Behind them, just visible as a spot on the grassy shoulder, was the file.

"Colin, wait, the picture," she cried. "You left it." She twisted around in her seat, trying to keep track of the tiny cream-colored object behind them. But in another second, it was gone.

"Oh, shoot, sorry." Colin reached over and patted her knee. "I must have dropped it." He accelerated slightly. "There's no place to get off here. Sorry," he repeated.

Hannah opened her mouth to protest, but a glance at Colin's blank face, his eyes fixed straight ahead, made her close her mouth with a snap. She faced forward and stared silently at the road unwinding before them.

CHAPTER 6

"Okay, it's coming up." Hannah sat forward in her seat as the highway sign loomed in front of them. KILGOUR, it read. "This is the exit." She pointed and Colin nodded. The light feeling had disappeared from the truck after the whole lake house argument. But at least the grim set was gone from his mouth. *He's just tired from the drive,* Hannah told herself. She was too. They'd both feel better when they got there.

Colin signaled and swung down the exit ramp. "Which way?" he asked at the bottom. The ramp ended at a forked road. There were no signs. No other cars, even. Just pine trees and on one side of the road, a closed-up restaurant with weathered boards tacked over the windows. Weeds grew up through the cracked asphalt parking lot and a signboard read SPEC L .99 WICH. On the other side of the road sat a tiny gas station with two pumps out front.

"Um . . ." Hannah unfolded the hand-drawn map. At the very bottom, a black curve indicated the highway they had just left—the exit was marked with a tiny *X*. She squinted at the faint black lines. The thing was hard to read. So different than a printed map. "Left, I think. It's not that clear."

"Damn it, I wish I had a GPS. So, is this the right way?" Colin indicated the road to the left.

"I don't know," Hannah admitted. "I tried to get Google directions, but it wasn't coming up." She looked around helplessly, the map on her lap. Colin exhaled through his nose and then swung the car around and pulled up in front of the little gas station. "I don't think this is open, Colin," she said. The little building was the size of a toolshed, the big front windows smeary.

Colin killed the engine. "Well, let's hope they are. We need some gas." He got out. "Go in and buy a road map while I fill up, okay? And tell them we want ten gallons of gas. I don't know how much it'll cost."

"You don't remember anything about how to get up there?" Hannah asked hopefully.

He frowned and shook his head. "I told you, Han, I was ten. I barely remember the place, much less how to get up there." He unhooked the gas pump. "How do you work this thing?" he muttered, examining the antique brass handle. Hannah left him winding a crank at the side of the gas pump and tried the cloudy glass door of the store. To her surprise, it opened.

A gaunt-faced guy in his thirties looked up from a stool by the window. A shock of ginger hair stuck out from under his dirty ball cap. The lights were off for some reason, which threw the tiny room into half gloom. On the scarred metal shelves, a few items were sparsely arranged: a bottle of engine oil, a package of Dr. Scholl's corn pads, a bottle of Prell shampoo. Near the counter, some tired candy bars sat in a rack next to a little spin rack of maps. Hannah sighed with relief.

Hannah felt the man's eyes on her as she examined the rack. Two different state maps and three county maps. "Um, what county are we in?" she asked the guy. Instead of answering, he plucked one of the maps from the rack and handed it to her in silence. Hannah shot a quick glance at his impassive face and decided not to ask for directions. "And ten gallons of gas too, please."

"Thirty-one fifty," the guy said and Hannah jumped with surprise. His voice was like that of a robot, deep and metallic with an odd vibration to it. Then Hannah noticed a small round hole at the base of his neck, covered with white mesh. She swallowed and held out the money, trying not to touch his hand.

He accepted the cash and then sat back on his stool and resumed staring into space as Hannah escaped through the door, map clutched in her hand.

"Did you figure it out?" she asked Colin. He nodded, setting the pump back in its holder.

"Yeah. It's a good thing too. You wouldn't want to run out of gas out here."

Hannah nodded and climbed into the truck cab. "It was weird in there," she said to Colin. "There was like nothing on the shelves."

Colin shrugged as he started up the engine. "They probably don't get a lot of business."

He pulled out. Hannah unfolded the new map on her knees. It rustled with reassuring crispness. "It looks like we want . . ." She brought the map closer to her eyes. "East. Would that be left?" She looked up at the road sign nearby. "So, I guess we want this one. Burnt Cabin Road." She blinked. "What a weird name."

"It's descriptive," Colin said dryly. He turned left and the highway quickly receded behind them, along with the familiar rush of cars. Patches of pinewoods flashed by, alternating with flat pastures on either side. The road was a gray chalk line drawn in the earth. Sodden haystacks reared up in the fields like boulders under the whitish sky. They passed a barn that looked as if it had caught on fire and a farmhouse long abandoned, the glassless windows gaping like blind eyes. No cars passed them either way, though they had been driving for almost half an hour.

Hannah stared out the window. The monotonous landscape made her feel half asleep, as if she was being hypnotized. The area was really desolate. She didn't know it was going to be like this.

A stop sign loomed ahead, the first turn since the gas station. Colin pulled up. The intersecting road was just as flat and lonely. A small black and white sign on a post read 51.

"Is this us?" Colin asked. Hannah scrabbled for her maps.

"Um . . ." She spread both maps out on her lap and tried to compare the two. But she couldn't match up any of the roads on the hand-drawn map with those on the county map. Hannah shook her head. "This map from the gas station is the same as

Google," she told Colin. "It doesn't have the roads up to the house on it. Weird."

"Let me see." He leaned over. Hannah gazed down at the top of his bright head.

"Well, we'd probably get even more lost if we were in New Zealand, right?" She tried for a light tone.

He glanced up. "Yeah," he said briefly and bent over the maps again. Hannah bit her lip.

Colin straightened up. "Okay, look, that's probably the lake." He pointed at a small splotch of blue in the middle of a vast tract of green spread over the middle of the map, near the highway exit they'd taken. "Let's just try to get there."

"So why do you think the roads from the homemade map aren't on the county one?" she asked.

Colin shook his head. "Maybe they're too small. Plus this map is like a hundred years old. All the roads are probably different now." He handed the maps back to Hannah. "My dad must have had the way up memorized," he said and threw the truck into drive again. "Let's just get up there. I'm sick of being in this car."

Hannah shot him a quick glance. His face was getting that drawn look again and there were lines around his mouth. He did look tired, and pale. "Okay," she said quickly. This wasn't going at all as planned. She stared at the hand-drawn map again. Maybe those two intersecting lines in the middle were the crossroads they were at now. If that was the case, they were almost there. "Left," she said, taking a chance.

Colin swung the car left. Here, a rough rock wall bordered the road for several miles, enclosing overgrown farm fields. Broken, rusty machinery was scattered across the landscape like mastodon skeletons. In the distance, Hannah could see a gaunt white farmhouse. But they were too far away to tell if anyone lived there or not. She shivered. Everything about this trip since they got off the highway was wrong. First Colin's bad mood, then the weird gas station, and now the desolate landscape. Into the back of her mind wiggled the faint worm of worry that this might have all been a mistake. But Hannah shoved that thought away firmly.

The rock wall ended and the car bumped onto dirt. Colin and Hannah looked at each other. "Guess this is where the paved road ends," Hannah said. She tried a tentative smile. Her heart lifted when Colin smiled back.

"Good thing I just got new shocks put on."

Heavy pinewoods lined either side of the road, making a tunnel of arcing boughs. This had to be it. There were all those woods around the house in the photo. "Colin, I think we're getting close." Her spirits rose a little. They'd get to the house and then everything would be fine. The ride was just stressing Colin out—that was all. They'd get to the house and unpack and take showers and a nap on some comfy old bed, all twined up in each other. Hannah hung on to this vision. She ran her finger along the triangles indicating woods on the old map. There were several more turns. She examined the county map again. None of these roads were on there. She flung the map in the backseat.

They turned down another dirt road and then a third. Hannah hoped they were going in the right direction—they hadn't seen a road sign since they left the crossroads. Not another car either. Colin drove steadily, silently. Gray shadows had appeared under his eyes.

Just tired, Hannah reassured herself, leaning forward in her seat. She could see an opening in the dense woods. "I think this is the turnoff here," she said.

Colin turned the car down the tiny dirt road. It was barely big enough to get the truck through. The pine boughs scraped the truck on either side, like reaching fingers. The road could barely be called a road—it was a rutted path. Weeds grew knee-high up the middle. Hannah clutched the door handle as Colin hung onto the steering wheel to keep it from flying out from his grasp.

Her mouth was dry. She licked her lips. Any minute she'd get her first glimpse of Pine House. Hannah kept her eyes fixed on the path, waiting to glimpse some kind of opening at the end. She glanced at Colin's face but his expression was unreadable.

Suddenly the woods opened up, pulling back on either side. "That's it!" Hannah couldn't keep the excitement from her voice. She grasped his sleeve as he stopped the car and turned off the ignition. They both stared through the windshield.

The house sprawled at the very edge of the lake—its clapboards gray like the sky. Bay windows jutted from the front, and elaborate scrolling dripped from every eave. In front of it spread what Hannah thought must have at one point been a lawn. Now the grass lay in luxuriant green swathes, crowding the foundation. Ivy wound its way up the rain gutters. Paint hung in shreds from the clapboards, and from where she sat Hannah could see dead leaves and twigs strewn across the porch. Her eyes followed the big wraparound porch over to the right corner. There was the broken railing, just like in the photo.

The worm of unease hatched earlier now uncoiled in her belly. *Not exactly a vacation paradise.* And it was so far off the road too. Hannah glanced over at Colin, but his face was blank as he sat behind the wheel. For a moment, she thought of telling him to just drive away, that this was obviously a mistake. They'd go back to the highway, find a motel for a couple days.

But then she looked back at the house. It was sitting patiently, waiting for her, as it already knew her decision. *Come here*, she could almost hear it whispering. She got out of the truck and slammed the door. The sound echoed in the silence. "Come on," she said to Colin. "Let's go in."

CHAPTER 7

Colin paused, just for an instant, and then followed Hannah up the path toward the house. Their feet crunched on the gravelly soil as the long grass caught at their ankles. Halfway up, Hannah stopped and inhaled. The air was heavy with the rich, rotting odor of lake mud, overlaid with the astringent scent of the pine needles that lay everywhere. A whip-poor-will called once from a nearby tree and then fell silent, as if thinking better of it.

Hannah looked up at Colin. "Do you remember it now?" she asked eagerly.

He shook his head. "No. It's like I'm here for the first time." He paused. "The smell, though. I do remember the smell. Like dead fish." His voice was flat.

Hannah squeezed his arm. "It's not so bad. The lake is gorgeous, don't you think?" She cast an arm toward the water and as if commanded, the sun broke through the clouds—lighting a million sparkles on the lake.

Colin looked around at the wild landscape. For the first time since their fight in the car, his face relaxed. "Yeah, it's not too bad."

She took Colin's hand and swung it a little as they walked together. Almost like they were married, Hannah thought, and they were about to go into their home together for the very first time.

She mounted the porch steps, her eyes already fixed on the front door, when suddenly she felt the top step give way under her foot and her hand slide out from Colin's. She gasped and arms flailing, managed to grasp the rickety banister.

"Careful!" Colin grabbed her around the waist. She clung to his shoulders as she pulled her foot out of the middle of the step, trying not to snag her jeans on the jagged edge.

"Nice welcome," she said. Colin and she stared down at the dark hole. The point of a rusty nail stuck out two inches from the rotted boards.

"Okay?" Colin asked. She nodded and he released her.

She laughed shakily. "I guess a lot of things are probably falling apart in this house."

"I guess so," Colin replied, a little grimly. He examined the front door, a huge carved wooden affair. The brass doorknob was rusty and crusted with age. He paused, then twisted and pushed.

Hannah's breath caught when the door swung open as if it had been oiled. "It's not locked."

Colin shrugged. They were standing on the threshold of a large, airy room. It was sparsely furnished with an old-fashioned wood-frame sofa and a few scattered armchairs, the high-backed kind with wings for your head. Weak sunlight filtered through a picture window on the opposite wall. A footlocker trunk sat underneath.

Hesitantly, Hannah stepped over the threshold. "I didn't know it was still all set up like this," she murmured to Colin. Her eyes darted around the room, trying to take in everything at once.

"Me neither," he said. His voice sounded abnormally loud. Hannah felt an irrational urge to shush him, as if they were disturbing someone.

The air was close and stuffy. Hannah walked over to the sofa. A book lay splayed open, facedown on the side table. It was *Middlemarch*, opened at page 210. Beside it was a coffee cup with a brown crust in the bottom. Hannah looked more closely. A lip mark still stained the rim. The sofa cushions were mashed in one corner, as if the reader had just gotten up for a second to answer the phone. Hannah backed away, bumping into one of the chairs. She jumped at the touch on her back and whirled around. *Jesus, this place was creepy.*

Hannah looked around the room again, her mouth cottony. A jigsaw puzzle sat on a card table in the corner, partially finished. On a tall oak coatrack behind the door hung a brown jacket and a yellow slicker. She looked down at the floor. Next to the door, a pair of galoshes sat, one toppled over the other. Dried mud clung to the heels. Hannah inhaled sharply and her palms grew clammy.

As if propelled against her will, she crossed the living room to an open doorway leading to the kitchen. She peered in. A cup and saucer sat on the table next to an empty plate. The chair was pushed back, with a flowered napkin draped over the seat. Dried mouse droppings were scattered on the table and floor. The white, metal-rimmed counters were lined with canisters labeled FLOUR, SUGAR, COFFEE, TEA. A teakettle stood on a front burner of the stove.

Hannah turned away from the scene. "Colin," she whispered. He didn't answer. He was standing at the picture window, one hand on the heavy orange and yellow drapes, staring outside. "Colin?" Her voice rose with a touch of hysteria.

"What?" He swung around, his face blurry, as if he'd been woken from a heavy sleep.

"Christ, Colin," she half whispered. "All of this stuff is here. Like your family just got up and walked away. I've never seen anything like this before." She pressed her hands to her mouth. She darted glances all around. Three closed doors led off a hallway at the other end of the room. She stared, waiting for one of them to open.

Colin shook his head. "I don't know why it's like this."

"Maybe we shouldn't stay." Hannah's voice sounded high and nervous, even to her own ears.

"Why not?" Colin's forehead creased. "We trekked all the way out here—we might as well stay."

"I don't know." She looked at the coffee cup by the couch. "It's just creepy to walk in and see everything laid out like this.

I thought things would be covered up and put away—stuff like that."

Colin shrugged. "What difference does it make?" He folded her into his arms. "It's my family's place. Of course we can stay. We'll just clean it up a little." He squeezed her shoulders. "Look, I know I was a little upset about coming up, but we're here now. Let's just relax, okay?"

His chest was comfortable and familiar, like her pillow at home. She wrapped her arms around his waist. The tension flowed out of her limbs. "Yeah, you're right."

"Good." He kissed her.

Hannah kissed him back and then disentangled herself from his arms. "I'm going to go freshen up."

"Okay," Colin replied, turning back to the window.

In the little dark hallway, Hannah cracked open the first door to find a white tiled bathroom. With relief, she darted inside. A mildewed shower curtain hung inside a claw-foot tub streaked with mineral stains. The toilet bowl was full of rusty water, but it looked usable. She didn't have a lot of choice anyway, she thought.

The sink—one of those old-fashioned ones with the separate hot and cold faucets—spurted warm, orange water at first, but then it changed to clear. Hannah splashed a handful on her face and looked around for a towel. A threadbare blue one hung on a hook near the sink. She pulled it off and wrinkled her nose at the musty smell. She dried her face on the hem of her shirt.

The medicine cabinet over the sink was a big metal box with a single small mirror set into the front. On impulse, Hannah swung it open and gazed at the bottle of generic aspirin and the packet of straight razors that sat alone on the metal shelves.

She came out of the bathroom and glanced toward the living room. Colin was no longer visible at the window. Quietly, Hannah opened the door next to the bathroom. She looked in on a simple bedroom, a large wooden bedstead neatly made up with a plain white spread. A pair of reading glasses perched on a nightstand, where more books were piled. The one tiny window above the bed showed the tops of pine trees clustered closely to the house.

Hannah swung the door closed and opened the one across the hall. It was a child's room—twin beds stood against each wall and a battered rug on the floor patterned with airplanes lay askew. In the corner by a window was a desk cluttered with pinecones, stones, and glass jars of twigs and dead grass.

Hannah turned away. She felt vaguely dirty. Resisting the impulse to glance over her shoulder, she hurried back down the hallway and through to the living room. The flood of light from the big window seemed very friendly and welcome all of a sudden.

She looked around. Colin was gone. "Colin?" she called. Her voice sounded oddly muffled and flat, bouncing off the walls of the room. Then she saw that a screen door on the other side of the room was open, flapping loose in the wind.

She went over to a short flight of spindly wooden stairs that led down to the little rocky beach. Hannah could see Colin standing off to the side, staring at something obscured by a big tangle of bushes.

She clopped down the stairs, which were sprinkled with sand. The lake spread out in front of her. Mist hung a few feet above the dark, glassy water, shrouding it heavily so that she could not see the opposite shore. The little beach was a jumble of sand and gray rocks. The water filtered through reeds poking up from the bottom before it lapped at the shore.

Hannah picked her way through the rocks, trying not to turn her ankle. She could see Colin's head and shoulders above the bushes. Panting a little, Hannah reached his side. "Hey," she said. She followed his eyes.

A moldy rowboat was pulled up on the shore. Hannah remembered seeing it in the photo. It looked as old as the house—the paint had long worn away from the soft-looking boards. A couple of planks laid across the middle served as seats, and a pair of oars were slung on the bottom.

Colin was holding his camera. As Hannah watched, he raised the camera to his face and pressed the shutter several times. He moved around to the other side and took a few shots there too. "Great shape," he said.

She squinted at the boat. "Yeah, it's okay."

He leaned over the edge and snapped a shot of the oars. Hannah put a hand on his back and he straightened up. "Let's go inside," he said, draping an arm around her shoulders. They headed back toward the house. "I'm starving."

Hannah looked back at the boat as they climbed the stairs to the house. A single piece of ragged rope trailed from the bow, the hemp prickly and dark with age. She shivered without knowing why.

CHAPTER 8

The back door slapped flatly behind them as Hannah followed Colin back into the house. "I'll grab the bags from the car," he said over his shoulder, his step brisk and confident again. Hannah imagined his figure disturbing the thick, still air of the house, like a rippling eddy in a sluggish stream.

"Okay."

His footsteps descended the porch stairs. Hannah stood still in the center of the floor, feeling a thin layer of grit in the bottom of her sneakers, the frayed laces pressing on her instep. The room was perfectly silent except for a fly buzzing and bumping against the window. It must have come in with them. Outside, Colin slammed the car door. But even that sound was muffled in the heavy air that shrouded the room.

Hannah suddenly felt the distance around them, the miles of woods separating them from the nearest house, from even one road. Her breath hitched and a wave of claustrophobia tightened around her throat. The rough gray walls of the room seemed to rise around her, enclosing her in a high box. What were they doing here? What had she done? Running away like this—lying.

Quickly she moved to the near window and, twisting the stiff latch, shoved the splintery frame upward with all her strength. It resisted, and then gave with a groan. Hannah pressed her face against the rusty screen, inhaling the rich mud and grass odor that wafted in along with the rushing noise of the wind in the pine trees. The silence became more ordinary and the tightness in her throat slowly loosened.

Hannah turned, blowing out her lips in a long exhale. *Okay, get a grip. It's all going to be okay—Colin seems fine now. And the place is nice, actually.* She examined the room more closely. The wide gray board walls were unpainted and darkened with age. Overhead, the ceiling arched, crisscrossed with exposed rafters. On each outside wall, wide windows stretched, facing the lake, so that the water seemed like it was going to lap right up to the edge of the floorboards. Who cared if it was a little strange? *Hannah, you're here, alone with your boyfriend for the first time, really alone, at Pine House, and nothing to do but just lie around, eat, swim, talk.*

Swiftly, before she thought too much about what she was doing, she crossed to the sofa, where *Middlemarch* sat open beside the stained coffee cup. In one motion, she picked up the book, slamming it shut, and shoved it under the couch. Anything to get rid of it fast. She grabbed the coffee cup and carried it through to the kitchen, where she dropped it into the sink. Then, back in the living room, she plumped the couch cushions, choking a little on the dust, and smoothed them with both hands.

She stood back and surveyed her work. *You'd never know anyone had ever been there,* she thought just as the outside door slammed. This was *her* house now—hers and Colin's. Whatever had gone on here before was over.

She looked up as Colin came into the room with the duffel bags over each shoulder. Sweat beaded his forehead. "Hot out." He looked around. "There's a nice breeze in here though."

Hannah smiled with satisfaction. "Where do you want to sleep?" The words sounded ordinary but she felt a shiver go through her as she followed Colin's broad back down the hallway toward the bedrooms. A little giggle of anticipation escaped her like a bubble, and Colin turned around, smiling. His eyes gleamed in the shadowy darkness.

"What?" His voice was low and teasing, as if he'd already guessed what she was thinking.

"Nothing." His face was very close to hers.

"Nothing," he teased, imitating her. He grabbed her around the waist with the suddenness of a snake strike. She giggled again, and he stopped the laugh by pressing his mouth to hers. Hannah leaned into the kiss. His arm circled her waist, pulling her in closely, and Hannah felt her heart quicken. His lips were firm and insistent. He pressed her against him, and she felt her head fall back. A doorknob was digging into her back. Feeling behind her, she twisted the smooth china knob. The door swung open, and they almost fell into the room beyond.

It was the room with the big bed. Hannah, eyes mostly closed, let Colin press her backward onto the mattress. She felt him leaning over her. Smiling, she stretched her arms over her head, waiting for him to clasp her hands and kiss her again. But his body grew still.

Hannah opened her eyes. Colin was leaning over her, but his eyes were fixed on the small window opposite the bed.

Hannah craned her neck back, but all she could see out the window were trees and gray sky. "Colin?" she murmured.

He looked down at her as if surprised to see her there. "Hmm?"

"Are you okay?" she asked carefully.

He shook his head a little and blinked. "Of course." But he rolled over to one side.

Hannah raised herself up on an elbow and looked around. There wasn't much to see. Books stacked beside the bed: some Jane Austen and a dictionary. A closed closet door. The white bedspread. That was all.

"Was this your parents' room?" she asked.

Colin shook his head. "I don't know. I guess so. I already told you like six hundred times, Han, I don't remember this place. Okay?"

Hannah sighed. "Sorry. I'm just curious, and I don't have anyone else to ask."

"Okay, let's forget it." Colin smiled his easy grin. "You're so gorgeous on that white quilt. Hang on." He climbed off the bed and disappeared down the hall for a moment, returning with his camera in his hand.

"Okay, let's see it," he said, his camera already at his eye. Hannah grinned and scooted backward on the bed until she was half propped against the pillows. She struck a pose, arms behind her head, hips twisted to the side.

"Nice." Colin snapped a few shots. "Very Hollywood bombshell."

Hannah snorted and flipped onto her stomach. "All us bombshells wear jeans and T-shirts with"—she looked down at the words on her shirt—"Reider High Mathlympics on them." She sucked in her cheeks and aimed a sultry look at the camera.

Colin zoomed in, the camera clicking in an insectile manner.

"Hey, not too close!" Hannah protested, holding her hands up in front of her face.

"What do you mean 'not too close'? Like this?" Colin put a knee up on the bed and leaned over. Hannah giggled a little as he advanced closer, still holding the camera. He clicked off another shot and moved closer. She pressed herself back against the pillows and reached for him.

Colin shoved the camera to one side and bent over her. She closed her eyes, relishing the hot, insistent pressure of his lips on hers. Before Colin, she didn't even know what a kiss was. Howard Mortenson freshman year didn't count. Kissing him was like having someone toilet plunge her mouth. And after that, no one . . . until Colin.

Too soon, Colin drew his head back. He stretched out on his side next to her, propping his head up with his hand. His blue eyes were soft and sparkling. The sun must have come out because a dapple of sunlight played on the wall behind him. "Are you happy we came up here?" he asked.

She nodded, rolling a little closer to him. "Yeah. I can't believe we made it, but I'm really happy." She burrowed her face into the hard muscles of his chest. She could hear his heart beating slow, strong thuds. Her muscles felt limp, as if her body were filled with honey. She gazed into Colin's face, lazily stroking the side of his stubbly cheek with the tips of her fingers, smiling. This felt good. It felt right, finally, after all the angst from earlier.

Colin moved an inch closer. "Han . . ." His breath blew softly against her cheek. "I . . ."

She felt herself tighten up. No. Not yet. It was too soon. She wasn't ready right now. She rolled away from Colin and slid off the bed. He sighed and flopped back on the pillows, staring up at the ceiling.

Hannah stood at the edge of the bed, trying to gauge his level of frustration, chewing her lip. A little moment of silence stretched out—familiar silence. This was the silence they'd been inhabiting since he first spoke those three words graduation night. "You want to get something to eat?" she offered after a long moment. She tried a little smile.

"Sure." He sighed and shoved himself off the bed.

Just a little more time. That was all she needed, she told herself as she followed Colin down the hallway.

CHAPTER 9

The light was growing dimmer as the sun declined behind the trees, and automatically, Hannah flicked the switch as they entered the kitchen. Nothing. She flipped it on and off again. "No electricity," she said to Colin as he systematically opened cabinet doors.

"Right, that makes sense. That means no fridge, too." Colin opened the cabinet over the sink with a particularly loud screech. "Baked beans?" He held up a can with a stained red and white label and examined the side. "Expired three years ago. Sounds great, right?"

"Sure. I'm starving." Hannah sat down at the table, trying to think. The adventure seemed very real now. "So, no lights. Um, do we have a flashlight?"

Colin was now rummaging through drawers. "Our phones have lights."

"Right, but I don't think that'll be enough. Do we seriously have no flashlights? It's going to be really dark soon." She tamped down a little twinge of fear as she spoke.

"How about this?" Colin's voice was triumphant. He turned from a deep drawer holding up a can opener in one hand and two grubby white candles in the other. "And matches, too."

"Great!" Hannah made herself sound enthusiastic. Pulling two blue-speckled bowls from one of the glass-fronted cabinets, she opened the can of beans with a few turns of the can opener, dumped it into the bowls and set them on the table. She paused. "Do you think the stove still works?"

"Maybe." Colin examined the gas grates. "We can always try. It's not electric, after all." He twisted one of the knobs but nothing happened.

"Try lighting it with a match." Hannah sniffed. "I can smell the gas coming out."

"Good plan. First we'll blow ourselves up, then we'll eat dinner. I like how you think, Han." Colin pulled a match from the box. "Stand back."

Hannah edged over as he touched the flame to the grate. Blue fire sprung up, and Hannah squealed. "Nice!" She grabbed their bowls of beans and scraped them into a saucepan. "At least we can have hot expired beans."

After a few minutes, she refilled their bowls and held her spoon out toward Colin. "A toast. To our very own vacation paradise," she said. "Sort of."

They clinked spoons, then dug into the sludgy beans, which looked like the leavings from a cement mixer.

Colin chewed manfully for a few moments. Hannah watched in silence. Then all of a sudden, they looked at each other and laughed. Hannah laughed so hard she had to lay down her spoon. Tears spurted from the corners of her eyes. Colin fell off his chair with a theatrical thump and lay spread-eagled on the floor.

"Oh my God," Hannah said weakly when her giggles had trailed off. She wiped her eyes. "Why are we eating this crap?"

"I have no idea." Colin sat up. "I need some real food. Let's go to town. Come on, the map's in the car."

Outside, dusk was falling. The screen door clapped behind them as they stepped out into the rich, loamy twilight air. Hannah stopped so suddenly that Colin almost ran into her from behind. "Oh, look." She pointed. Across the lake, the sky was streaked with deep blue and violent orange so pure, it was almost painful to look at. In between the streaks burned delicate rose and clear, perfect violet. The sunset was reflected in the lake itself, blurred and reaching to the very edges of the water. The pine trees surrounding the lake made a dark, jagged boundary between the water and the sky, with the woods pressing in all around them.

Colin glanced up. "Yeah, pretty," he said without stopping. He climbed into the truck, and Hannah hurried after him, her sneakers gritting on the gravel of the overgrown drive.

Colin was already bent over the county map, the dome light shining down weakly on the yellowed paper. "Okay, assuming this blue spot is the lake, then the nearest town should be . . ." He traced his finger down the page. "Nowhere?" He looked at

Hannah. "Looks like we might have to go all the way back to the highway for food."

"That's like forty miles!" Hannah grabbed the homemade map from the dash. "There was a town, it's marked—here." She stabbed a tiny dot, labeled OXTOWN. "It's probably too small for the big map."

"Assuming it's still in existence," Colin muttered. "Okay, it doesn't look too far, maybe . . ." He measured the distance from the highway with his fingers, then the distance from Pine House to town. "Like two or three miles."

"Oh, that's nothing." Hannah settled back into the passenger seat as Colin folded the map and started the truck down the bumpy road.

Path *was more like it. Woods. Pine trees, more pine trees. Big trunks, little trunks. Branches. Totally isolated.*

The thought popped unbidden into her head, and she shoved it away. There was nothing wrong with being alone. *It's romantic,* she told herself. The road was mainly two wheel ruts with weeds growing up the center. The woods themselves were already a black mass, even though the sky still held streaks of sunset overhead. Hannah stared into the trees until her eyes hurt, trying to pick out even the tiniest comforting detail, like a rabbit nibbling grass, or a deer. But there was nothing—just darkness, with black branches stabbing the sky. Hannah shuddered, looking away. For what seemed like a long time, she watched the tunnel of branches in front of them.

It seemed to be taking a lot longer from the house to the road than Hannah remembered. But finally, she saw a faint strip of gray at the end of the tunnel, which widened rapidly. The trees grew sparser, and Colin bumped the car onto the main road and turned right.

Hannah realized she was sitting forward in her seat, one hand gripping the door handle. She sank back, surprised to feel a little frisson of relief in her chest. The truck wheels thrummed reassuringly on the slate gray asphalt. The road was small, with just one narrow lane on each side. In front of them, the double yellow line unspooled like a ribbon.

They were silent. Hannah gazed out the window again. Beside her, Colin drove smoothly, efficiently. They passed overgrown pastures lined with decaying rail fences. Here and there, a skinny cow stood morosely over a feed trough. Smudges of dark trees divided the fields, which should have been waving with six-foot corn at this time of year. But most appeared to have never been planted and were choked with waist-high weeds.

Farmhouses drooped beside their fields in the deepening twilight. A huge mansion, like a decaying wedding cake, stood on a little rise with an equally grand barn in the back. But glassless windows gaped like blinded eyes. Loose clapboards hung from the walls and lay strewn on the ground where they'd fallen.

There was something missing. But she couldn't quite figure it out. Then she got it. "Colin, you know what's weird?"

Colin jerked a little, as if awakening from a daydream, and glanced over. "Hmm, what?"

"No other cars. No one outside. No one. We've been driving

straight on this one road, and we haven't seen a single person or car since we left the road to Pine House . . ." She looked at the odometer. "Seven miles ago."

Colin's brow creased. "There've been cars."

"No, Colin, there hasn't. Not even one other car." It was like they were the only people left on earth. Which was stupid of course. The place was just really depressing.

Just then another truck appeared, coming toward them. An early-model black Ford, the kind Hannah's grandfather used to drive. Colin pointed triumphantly. "There, see? I told you there were other cars."

They both watched the Ford approaching. The paint was dull and the bumper cracked. The truck loomed in their windshield, then whooshed by, a stone-faced man in a feed cap at the wheel.

Hannah settled back in her seat. The sight of the other driver should have made her feel better, but somehow, she wasn't comforted. She stared out the window at a scummy little pond, then at a group of crows picking a raccoon carcass on the shoulder. There was nothing ahead of them but more open country. She shifted around. "Shouldn't we be there by now?"

Colin glanced at the odometer and lifted his eyebrows. "Thirteen miles. I didn't realize we'd gone so far."

Hannah reached in the back for the old map. "You said it looked like just a couple of miles from the house." She traced the line Colin had pointed out and tried to mark it using her thumb.

Colin shrugged. "Maybe it's not drawn to scale. It's just homemade."

Hannah folded her hands over her stomach, which gave a loud gurgle. "Well, I'm hungry, it's dark, and we're really far away from food. And the highway exit is forty miles the opposite direction too. That means we're forty miles from French fries. It's time for emergency measures." She leaned forward and snapped open the glove compartment, riffling around among oil-change receipts and yellowing parking tickets. "Ah!" She held up a wrinkled box triumphantly.

Colin glanced over. "Stale Mike and Ikes?"

"Hell, yes." Hannah excavated a few cracked red candies from the box and, leaning over, popped them in Colin's mouth.

"Mmm." He worked his jaw with some difficulty. "Chewy."

Hannah grinned at him. "Yeah. I like them best with dust." She rubbed a green one against her shirt and ate it.

Colin braked abruptly in the middle of the road and Hannah sat up. "What are you doing?"

He spun the wheel and turned around, backing up and then threw the truck into drive. He accelerated back toward Pine House. "This is way too much hassle. I propose we go back to the house, eat our expired baked beans, take these inside"—he held up the Mike and Ikes—"to finish in bed." He grinned at Hannah, bathing her in the full force of his high-wattage smile.

She bit her lip as a delicious shiver ran from her neck to her fingertips. "That sounds like a great idea." She squeezed his knee under the dashboard and watched the road thrumming by ahead of them.

CHAPTER 10

Hannah woke by degrees the next morning. First the gray light filtering in through her eyelids. Then the sense of warmth encasing her from head to toe, and the awareness of Colin cradling her from behind, one arm draped around her middle. The room around them was silent—the one small window shrouded with the flat early morning fog. Hannah could feel the layers of silence pressing in on her from each room in the house, then the silence in the woods around them and in the countryside out beyond that.

She kept very still, relishing the rise and fall of her boyfriend's slow, regular breathing against her back, then shifted carefully to face Colin. He lay peacefully on his side, eyes closed, golden stubble glinting on his cheeks and chin. She stared at his high, sunburned cheekbones and the light sprinkling of freckles on his nose for a long moment before whispering, "Colin."

"Hrrm?" he mumbled without moving.

"Colin, are you awake?" she whispered a little louder.

He wrapped his arm around her neck and pulled her into his chest. "Hmm. Shh. Han . . ." His voice trailed off.

Hannah willed herself to go back to sleep. But she was wide-awake now, and her feet were hot and sweaty, like they always were when she stayed in bed too long. So after a minute, she slowly disentangled herself from his embrace and slid out from under the covers. Colin turned on his other side, mumbling something indistinct, and hugged the pillow as Hannah padded from the room.

The big living room seemed to regard her with serene calm, bathed in a pearly diffuse light. Hannah put her hand on a checked curtain and peered through the glass, trying to see the lake. The fog hung like a white shroud though, allowing only a view of the rough, sandy beach, with the rowboat sitting on one side.

In the kitchen the remains of their baked bean dinner from the night before still lay spread on the table. Hannah swept the dishes into the sink. No unloading the dishwasher here. No packing lunches. No grocery shopping.

As if on cue, her cell rang, the noise bone-jarring in the silence. Hannah looked around for it wildly and spotted it lying by her place at the table. She grabbed it up before it could ring again and hurried onto the porch.

Outside, the damp air was rich with the odor of lake mud and rotting reeds. Hannah flicked open the phone without looking at the screen. "Hello?"

"Hi, honey." Mom's voice came from the other end.

Hannah's heart stuttered. She glanced around quickly, as if expecting to see her mother standing at the edge of the gravel drive. "Hi, Mom." She sank down slowly on the edge of the splintery porch step. The hole she'd almost fallen through yesterday stared back at her.

"How's work going?" Mom asked. "We've been missing you here. David . . ." Her voice crackled and faded out, then in again. "Han? Han?"

Hannah glanced at the screen. One bar. "Shoot, hold on, Mom," she almost shouted into the receiver. She got up and walked down onto the overgrown lawn, holding the phone in the air, watching the screen. Really it was amazing there was any cell reception out here at all. One bar, then two, and then none. She stood at the side of the house near a falling-off gutter. "Mom? Mom?"

"What, honey?" Her mother sounded like she was shouting through a bucket. "I'm having trouble—" A burst of static interrupted her words. Hannah held the phone away from her ear, wincing.

"Mom!" she shouted. "Listen, the reception's bad. But I'm fine, everything's fine."

Another burst of static. She could hear her mother faintly saying something. Then the line went dead.

Hannah set the phone down on the edge of the porch, then leaned back against the cold, damp metal of the gutter. Weeds wet with dew brushed her ankles, leaving behind a trail of tiny green seeds. She tried to ignore the twist of emptiness in her middle, picturing David, waking up this morning and looking in her room, seeing the bed empty. She thought of his mouth, turned down in disappointment, and his sad little eyes.

She exhaled, forcing herself to focus on the lake in front of her. The water was visible now as a glassy, flat sheet, hung with a curtain of fog that stopped a few feet above the surface of the water, as if someone had rubbed an eraser through the landscape. Hannah squinted, trying to estimate how far the opposite shore was. *A mile? A half mile?* Far enough that the pine trees were visible only as an indistinct mass. In the eastern sky, the sun was a silver disk, steadily burning through the moisture.

Her skin felt coated with sweat and grime from yesterday and she had yet to take a shower. The water would be so cool and refreshing. On impulse, she slipped around to the back of the house. Here, the little beach lay spread out—the rough yellow sand damp from the night and strewn with dark branches and stones. In the water on either side, the reeds clustered, whispering together. As Hannah watched, a loon rose from the water. It called plaintively before diving under again.

She glanced back at the sleeping house. No movement at the windows. The back door was tightly shut. Quickly, she skimmed her T-shirt over her head and slid her gym shorts down to her ankles. She ran toward the water, feeling extremely exposed, and was sure that Colin had come to the back door. He was probably standing there, laughing at the sight of her running in her underwear. But when she plunged in and turned around, the back porch was still empty.

The cold dark water enveloped her skin like silk. Under her toes, mud squished. A reed brushed her calf, and she thought fleetingly of water snakes. *Don't be such a wimp.* It was colder than she expected, but she forced herself to wade deeper into the water as the chill worked its way into her bones. When she was up to her chest, she swam a little back and forth, churning her arms and kicking vigorously, trying to warm up. After a minute, the water didn't feel quite as cold. Hannah flipped over on her back. It felt very adventurous, being out here alone. The trees on the shore loomed over her field of vision like giant towering sentinels.

The screen door slapped behind her, and Hannah turned to see Colin standing on the porch, his hair sticking up. He wore nothing but his boxers and for a minute, Hannah could hardly breathe at the sight of his broad, golden chest and thick arms. She waved one arm in the air and paddled close enough to stand. "Come on in!"

He didn't move, so Hannah called again. "Colin! The water's great!"

"Awesome," he said, but his voice had an automatic quality as he stared past her at the water, his arms crossed on his chest.

Hannah swiped some of the wet hair out of her face. "What are you waiting for? Scared?" She laughed.

Colin laughed too, a bit hollowly. "Very funny. I'm just working up to it." He took a couple deep breaths, and then swung his arm back and forth a few times before walking slowly into the water. He seemed to relax as the water reached his chest. "Damn, it's cold."

He swam awkwardly in a circle, while Hannah floated on her back again, staring up at the white sky. The sun was burning stronger through the clouds. Now the fog hung above the water in thin wisps. Spirit vapors. That's what her grandmother used to call it. She glanced over. Colin looked like a disembodied head floating on the surface of the water. His hair was pasted to his forehead. "Come here," he said, swimming over. He lifted her easily in his arms as she wrapped her legs around his waist and her arms around his neck.

This close, she could see the individual water droplets that sparkled like diamonds on his tanned, wet face. "Mmm, you're so warm," she said, squeezing closer to him. Maybe she should tell him now. Right now. This could be the moment. She pressed herself closer to him, looked right into his broad, open face. He gazed back encouragingly. Then she dropped her eyes. It was like he was looking right through her skull. She knew he was thinking about it. And he knew she was thinking about it.

Colin released her, and she clung to him weightlessly, her legs still twined around his waist. He smoothed the wet hair off her forehead with both hands. "Love you." His voice was so low she had to lean forward to hear it.

Hannah hesitated. Colin sensed it immediately and twisted away from her. Just like in the bedroom yesterday. Her legs released his waist, and he swam a few feet, his back to her. She could tell by the set of his shoulders that he was upset. Her stomach felt sick. Again! What was the matter with her? *Relax, for God's sakes! Just say it!*

She swam up to him and held on to his broad shoulders from behind. The skin felt slick and slippery, like a seal's. "Colin . . . listen . . ." She pulled on his shoulders until he turned around. "I'm sorry." She hugged him, and after a minute, he hugged her back. Hannah tried a smile. "Can we just have a good time? I really, really want to remember this. Our last time together before you leave."

"That's a little dramatic, don't you think?" His voice was light, but she could hear the hurt still lingering underneath. He swam away from her toward the center of the lake, doing a serious crawl with proper breathing.

Hannah swallowed. Okay, no problem. She'd dealt with his moods before. She'd get him, she thought. Smiling to herself and taking several deep breaths, she ducked her head under the water and opened her eyes.

Before her floated a murky green world, with dark reeds waving at the bottom and the sunlight filtering through the thick water. Ahead, she could see Colin's body moving through the water, his legs kicking steadily.

She swam toward him and when she was close, dove a little deeper, then reached up and grabbed one of his ankles, pulling as hard as she could.

His ankle was all hard bone and sinew under her fingers. His leg kicked wildly, and she just barely managed to hang on. The force of the kicking swung her back and forth as if she were a shark clamped onto his leg. Her lungs were aching. She released his foot and kicked swiftly toward the surface of the water.

Hannah burst through the surface, raking her hair out of her eyes and already grinning. But she recoiled at the sick look on Colin's face. His skin was almost gray. Then, as she watched, the gray was slowly replaced by a flush.

"Colin, are you okay?" She reached out to touch him. "I'm sorry. I was just playing around."

He blinked rapidly several times. "Oh, yeah. Yeah, I'm fine." He smiled back, but it looked forced. "I was just startled, that's all." Abruptly, he turned and began swimming back toward the shore, his arms and shoulders moving in the same clumsy crawl.

"Colin, what . . . ?" But he didn't turn around. For a few moments, Hannah remained alone in the center of the lake, treading water. Then she followed, wading back through the muddy reeds near the shore and up onto the beach.

"Hang on," Colin said over his shoulder as he disappeared into the house. He reappeared a moment later, carrying two old blue towels. He handed her one, then rubbed himself with the other, facing away from her toward the trees. Hesitantly, Hannah touched his shoulder. He turned around. She was relieved to see that his face looked normal.

The morning air was growing warmer and brighter as the sun burned through the clouds. The wind blew lightly, carrying the sharp scent of the pine trees. "What was going on back there?" Hannah asked.

Colin took a deep breath and smiled a little with his lips closed. "It's nothing." He plucked Hannah's towel from her hands and draped it around her shoulders. She clutched the rough terry cloth close.

Colin sank down on the beach. After a moment's hesitation, Hannah sat down next to him. The gritty sand was cold under her rear. She stared at the ground in front of her. A large ant was trying to carry away a dead dragonfly. "Sorry I overreacted back there," Colin said.

Hannah nodded, trying to sift some sand between her fingers. This wasn't really the sifting kind though and just sort of fell in clumps.

Colin cleared his throat. "I guess I never told you that I hate swimming."

Hannah looked over at him sharply. He was digging a short stick into the damp sand in front of him. His cheeks were a little pink.

Hannah put a hand on his back. She could feel the gooseflesh under her palm. "I didn't know that," she said softly.

Colin nodded still looking down. "Yeah. Ever since I was little. I mean, I know how, of course. But I don't like it. I don't know why. I just hate the water." He dug the stick deeper into the sand and then abruptly threw it into the reeds.

"But you swam today," Hannah pointed out.

Colin shrugged. "Yeah, I know. I came out and saw you there and you looked so cute and like you were having so much fun and . . . I don't know, I just thought I'd try it." He looked over at her for the first time. "Guess it didn't work out so well."

"Guess not." Hannah rolled her eyes comically. "So, why do you hate swimming?"

"I don't know," Colin said. "It's just one of those things I always avoided. My parents thought it was dangerous anyway. They got nervous every time I even came near a pool or a lake or anything."

"God, that's crazy. I guess all parents have weird hang-ups, though." Hannah thought for a second. "I mean, when I was little, my mom was afraid of toads."

"Toads?" Colin asked incredulously.

Hannah nodded. "She'd read somewhere that they were poisonous. So anytime David or I found a toad in the yard, we'd bring it in and put it on the kitchen table, then hide until she found it. It was really funny watching her run around trying to sweep it up into the dustpan."

Colin mock-punched her on the arm. "Hannah Taylor! I thought you never did anything bad in your entire life."

"Until I met you, that was it. Now I'm lying to my mom and running away from home." She grinned at him. "And it's pretty fun too." She dusted the sand off her rear as she got to her feet.

"Oh here, let me help you with that." Colin swiped at her rear helpfully and then gave her a squeeze through her wet underwear.

"Thanks, thanks." Hannah laughed. "I couldn't handle that by myself." She climbed the stairs to the house but stopped short as they entered the living room. Through the doorway into the kitchen, they could see a large crow perched on the edge of the kitchen sink, pecking busily at the solidified baked bean remains.

At the sound of their voices, the crow looked up, cawed loudly, as if they were interrupting and leisurely spread its wings, soaring out through the open kitchen window.

Hannah looked at Colin. "At least the bird likes baked beans."

Colin snorted laughter, nodding. "Let's go find the town."

CHAPTER 11

Hannah settled back in the passenger seat of the truck and rolled the window all the way open. Her skin felt sleek and freshly scrubbed after her postswim shower. She relished the sharp air that ruffled the artfully messy braids she'd spent a laborious fifteen minutes constructing. The endless pine trees and deserted pastures around them seemed flat and undramatic this morning, more run-down than ominous. The same skinny cows still stood at the same feed troughs, and the lonely strip of asphalt was still empty.

Colin drove fast and confidently with one elbow cocked out the window and the breeze fanning his golden hair. "I'm starving," he half shouted over the wind as they rocketed down the road. "I swear to God, if we don't find this town and get some real food, I'm going to pull over and eat one of those cows. Raw."

"Delicious." Hannah rolled her eyes at him and snapped on the radio, dialing through a few stations. Static, static, a voice reading grain prices, static, some sort of religious sermon, then an old-time country station way down at the end of the dial.

"Hey, who were you talking to this morning?" Colin asked, tapping his fingers on the wheel.

Hannah started a little. "I thought you were sleeping."

"I was kind of drifting in and out. The walls are thin in that place. Was it your mom?"

She sighed and nodded. "She bought it—about me working with Laurie, I mean. I feel bad though. I hate lying to her. And leaving her with all the work."

Colin reached over and took her hand from where it lay in her lap. "Hey, babe, come on." He intertwined his fingers with hers. "It's not like you do this all the time. You're like the most responsible person I know. So for once, you cut out for a few days. It's worth it—it's for us."

"I know. But David, too. He probably thinks I've abandoned him." She swallowed and withdrew her hand.

"Believe me, he's fine." Colin braked for a squirrel scampering across the road. "Didn't you say the neighbor was watching him while your mom was at work?"

"Yeah," Hannah said slowly.

"And he loves walking that dog. So he's totally okay. Stop freaking out. Anyway, look, we made it." He pointed at a collection of small buildings approaching and glanced at the odometer. "Twenty-five miles. We weren't even close last night."

Colin slowed down as the tall oak trees slid by outside the windows. Hannah sat up, thumping her feet to the floor, and stared out the window. Oxtown seemed to be composed of a one block Main Street lined with turn-of-the-century buildings and an additional smattering of decaying frame houses behind. A Chevy with a broken tailpipe and a riding lawn mower were the only vehicles parked at the curb. The sidewalks were mostly empty. Halfway down the street, an old woman sat on a bench under an awning, digging through her purse. Colin turned into one of the parking spots and killed the engine.

"Wow. Did we take a wrong turn and wind up in South Beach?" He raised his eyebrows.

Hannah giggled. "Yeah—that would be no." She opened her door. "Come on. We're here at least."

Colin shrugged. "Yeah, let's check it out." He got out, pocketing the keys.

Joining hands, they began wandering up the cracked sidewalk. Most of the storefronts were empty, with fading FOR LEASE signs propped in the windows. Here and there, the ghosts of the former stores still remained: a sign reading KOLAR'S PHARMACY with a drawing of a druggist's mortar and pestle on one corner. LEHR'S MEAT AND GROCERY had a rusted grill out front but soap coated the windows. Most of the storefronts though were completely erased, transforming the Main Street into a death march of blank plateglass windows and peeling paint.

Hannah stopped and peered into one window that looked like it might have been a gift shop. The grimy gray carpeting inside was scattered with a few crushed silk flowers. White aluminum shelves swayed precariously from the walls. One near the front had fallen over. Random scraps of paper, a couple clothes hangers, and, near the front, a CLEARANCE—EVERYTHING MUST GO sign littered the floor.

Hannah glanced over at Colin and raised her eyebrows. "Cheery," she said.

"Yeah, bustling." He squeezed her hand and pointed down the block where a few cars were parked. "Look, at least something's open down there."

They passed a few widely spaced wood-frame houses. The tiny lawns were mostly bare dirt. In front of one, two blond-haired children were playing in an empty kiddie pool. They stopped as Hannah and Colin passed and stared with wide blue eyes.

"Hi there," Hannah said as they passed. The children did not reply. Hannah looked back a few yards later. They were still standing, staring after them. Hannah faced forward fast. "Okay. They must not get a lot of pedestrians around here," she murmured to Colin. "This place is totally depressing."

"Yeah, well, think about it," Colin said. "Where the hell do people work around here? There's no factories or plants, just farms. And farming doesn't make anyone rich."

"I know, but this is so sad." Hannah pointed to a large town square to their right. Gracious oak trees still towered over peeling wooden benches, but the grass around them was brown and neglected. "Doesn't that look like a Norman Rockwell painting gone bad?"

"And check this out." Colin pointed to a storefront they were just then passing. The big glass display windows were broken, with the glass littering the sidewalk. "Someone should come clean this up." He sidestepped a particularly jagged piece.

"This didn't just happen," Hannah said. Birds had built nests on the empty shelves. More broken glass was strewn on the floor.

"Okay, food ahead," Colin announced. They'd reached the end of the block where two battered pickups and a station wagon were parked in front of a café with a moldy yellow awning stretching overhead. EAT N'MEET read the sign. Broken venetian blinds slanted crazily at the windows and covered the door.

"Great," Hannah said. The stale candy of the night before was just a distant memory, and her stomach was so empty, it felt like it was turning in on itself. "I need some hash browns stat."

"I'm guessing you can have that." Colin indicated a hand-lettered sign in the window, which trumpeted BREAKFAST ALL DAY! $3.75 SPECIAL!

"Oh, wow, three seventy five. Are you treating?" Hannah teased. "Big spender."

"Just don't let it get around. I won't be able to keep the chicks away." Colin pushed the door open and a bell jingled.

The air inside was hot and still and reeked of sour mop water. In one window an old air-conditioner worked fitfully, while overhead, a few ceiling fans lazily stirred the thick air. At a Formica counter along one wall, a sunken-cheeked elderly man hunched over a bowl. A fat paperback was held open by a butter knife beside him. The only other inhabitant was a pale woman with a straggly brown ponytail sitting at a table near the front window. She was dreamily smoking a cigarette, a full ashtray in front of her.

At the back, some plain pine shelves held groceries. All around on the walls were black-and-white pictures of stern-faced farmers posing next to new Model T's and grainy snapshots of people seated around long picnic tables loaded with food. The place was so quiet Hannah could hear the scrape of her sneakers on the gritty wood floor. Beside her, Colin let the door close behind him with infinite care.

A man who must be the café owner bustled over to them. He seemed to be composed entirely of circles: round face, big round body, short fat arms and legs. He was the only cheerful person in the place—maybe because he was also the only business open in town.

"Help you?" he asked pleasantly.

"We were going to have breakfast?" Colin said. The ponytailed woman looked around at the sound of his voice. Hannah shifted a little under her stare.

The man nodded and pointed to a booth under the air conditioner, handing Hannah two sheets of paper encased in limp plastic. Colin slid in and leaned back in the booth on the other side and looked around expansively. "This place is classic. Like something from *Deliverance*."

Hannah raised her eyebrows. "Thanks for that reference. I feel so much better now." The air conditioner dripped steadily onto the tabletop. Hannah pulled a handful of flimsy paper napkins from the smeary metal holder and shoved them under the drip. "Should I be scared of the food here?"

Colin examined the tiny menu. "Definitely not. If you get sick, we can just play doctor."

Hannah laughed aloud and reached across the table to smack his shoulder.

"*Shhh,*" Colin stage-whispered. "You're disturbing that man's meal." He nodded meaningfully.

Hannah followed his eyes to the counter where the elderly man was scowling at them over his soup. "Oops," she whispered, opening her eyes wide as they both collapsed into giggles.

They were interrupted by a voice above them.

"Can I get you folks?" The round counterman had appeared at their table with a small pad of paper in one sausage-like hand and his dingy apron straining around his middle. MIKE read his name tag.

Hannah scanned the menu quickly. It wasn't hard since there were only about five items on it. "Um, can I get the Farmer's Friend, please, scrambled, with hash browns? And coffee."

Colin held out his menu. "I'll go for the western omelet. Looks good."

"Oh it is," Mike said, his hand reaching out for Colin's menu. "My mom's recipe—" He stopped suddenly.

Hannah and Colin glanced at each other. There was a brief, uncomfortable pause. Mike stared at Colin as if frozen. Colin cleared his throat politely and held the menu out a little farther.

Mike jumped and offered Colin a weak smile. "I'll get your order," he mumbled before hurrying away.

Hannah raised her eyebrows at Colin. "What was that?"

"I have no idea." Colin shook his head. "Maybe he was struck by my incredible good looks." He drummed his fingers on the sticky tabletop.

Hannah looked around. The woman with the brown ponytail had let the cigarette between her fingers burn down to a stub. The man at the counter had returned to his soup and was slowly scraping his bowl. The soft *scree* of the metal spoon on the porcelain raised the hair on Hannah's arms. She resisted the urge to cover her ears. Instead, she leaned across the table and picked up Colin's hand, entwining her fingers with his.

"So, what do you want to do today?" she asked.

"Do you even need to ask?" He waggled his eyebrows suggestively and under the table, she felt his foot press her leg.

"Oh my God, you're terrible. I can't believe you're playing footsie with me here in this nice, wholesome place." She extended her own foot and rested it in his lap and then sat upright fast, banging her knee on the underside of the table as Mike appeared with their food.

"Here you go." The counterman's cheerful tones rang above them as he set the plates down. Colin was choking back laughter, and Hannah shot him a dirty look while trying to simultaneously smile at Mike.

"Thanks," Colin said pleasantly, and picked up his fork.

Mike remained standing at the side of their table though, wiping his hands on his apron. He wet his lips. "Sorry about my reaction a few minutes ago. It's just that you are the spitting image of a boy who used to come with his family a few summers back."

Colin's mouth was already full of omelet. He swallowed. "My family did used to come up here, but not since I was a kid. About ten years ago."

"Oh? I must be remembering wrong. Getting old, you know." Mike picked up Hannah's empty water glass. "Not too many people up here the last few years, that's for sure. Not since the chemical plant closed." He waggled Hannah's glass. "More water, dear?"

She shook her head, and he hurried away on his short, round legs.

After their surprisingly tasty breakfast, Colin shoved a ten under his plate, and they rose, nodding to Mike at the counter.

They had just reached the car, the empty town stretching all around them, when Colin smacked his forehead with his palm. "Damn it! Groceries!"

Hannah stopped short. "Oh my God. I can't believe we were right there and forgot to buy anything."

Colin unlocked the passenger door. "Just wait here, I'll run back."

A few minutes later, he appeared at the truck window and stuffed a paper bag in behind the seats.

"What'd you get?" Hannah sat up and peered into the bag as he started the engine.

"The usual—some bread, peanut butter, that sort of thing." He accelerated out of the parking space and down the empty street.

"Good-bye, creepy town!" Hannah shouted behind her as they roared off. She turned around and settled in her seat just as her cell rang.

"Oh my God, what if that's Mom again?" she gasped, digging in her pocket.

Colin glanced over. "I can't believe there's service out here."

"Just my luck," Hannah muttered. She pried the phone out of her jeans and glanced at the screen. "Laurie." She sighed with relief. She flicked open the phone.

"Hey, I was so scared you were my mom," she said.

"Well, your mom is standing right here next to me," her friend's dry voice said on the other end.

Hannah's heart briefly stopped until she heard Laurie snort with laughter.

"You almost gave me a stroke," she shouted into the phone. Colin put a hand over one ear.

"I needed a little levity in my day."

Hannah could hear shuffling, as if Laurie were moving things aside. "Yeah, how's the chemistry library going?" She switched the phone to her other ear and stared out the window. They were passing the big house with the falling-off clapboards. The windows still looked like staring eyes.

"I'm sitting here in the hallway, looking at about five hundred boxes."

Hannah winced. "I thought you were going to have help for that job."

"I did. You," Laurie said pointedly.

Hannah winced. "I'm really sorry about that. It was just this crazy thing. I didn't think about it, for like the first time in my life." She glanced over at Colin who was tapping out a rhythm on the steering wheel. He nodded encouragingly. "Did you get someone else to help?" Hannah went on.

She heard Laurie sigh. "Yeah, don't worry. My cousin wanted to crash with us for a few days, so my dad's making him help. I'm just being a bitch because you're on vacation with your boyfriend and I'm moving a thousand copies of the *Journal of the Annals of the American Chemistry Society*. You know I'd do the same thing as you if I could."

"I know," Hannah mumbled.

"So how's it going anyway?" Laurie went on. She was puffing a little. "How is it being with Colin all this time? Is it great? Is it weird? Did you tell him you love him yet?"

"It's . . . great," Hannah said, glancing at Colin. "More great than weird. And . . . no on the other thing. But things are going really, really well."

Laurie squealed a little, and Hannah grinned.

"That's so awesome," Laurie said. "Is the house nice?"

Hannah licked her lips. "The house is . . . different. It takes a little getting used to. Oh, and there's no electricity. I'm shocked there's cell reception out this far—it's pretty spotty."

"Yeah, I was sure I wasn't going to get you." There was the sound of male voices in the background. Laurie said something indistinguishable to them and came back. "Look, the mover guys need me. Don't worry about your mom—I've got your back if she calls."

"Thank you, thank you," Hannah told her. "You're the best friend ever. Next time I escape anywhere, you're coming with me."

"Damn straight." Laurie hung up.

Hannah clicked the phone closed in her fist and glanced over at Colin. A little silence filled the cab of the truck. Colin continued tapping his fingers on the wheel.

"So . . . you told Laurie it was going great." He glanced at her, a little smile playing around the corners of his mouth.

"Well, I told her that because it's true." She reached over and squeezed his knee. "Even if things are kind of strange around here, it's still amazing being away with you."

Colin didn't answer. Instead he leaned way over, and keeping one eye on the road, kissed Hannah quickly on the neck. A shiver tingled down her spine. "Drive a little faster, would you?" she murmured.

CHAPTER 12

Scree! The ancient bolt pulled back with a screech, flaking bits of rust onto the overgrown grass. Hannah peered over Colin's shoulder into the blackness of the shed. A strong odor of damp wood and mold wafted out at them.

"Maybe you shouldn't go in." Hannah backed away. "What if there are bats?"

He rolled his eyes at her. "The door was bolted. How're the bats going to get in?" He stepped over the threshold.

Hannah clutched his sleeve "It's totally black in there," she said. Suddenly she stopped. "Wait!" She clapped her hand to her pocket. "I can't believe I didn't remember this last night." She dug in her jeans and pulled out a tiny flashlight at the end of her keychain.

Colin took the little purple object and turned it over a few times in his palm. "Thanks," he said dryly. He shone the weak beam into the darkness, illuminating a stack of metal buckets and a pitchfork standing near the front.

It was on the ride home from town that Hannah had gotten the idea they should check out the old shed. Now though, as she scratched one of the many mosquito bites dotting her ankles, she thought maybe this hadn't been such a great idea. "Colin, let's just go for a walk—" she started to say but her words were cut off when Colin shook her hand off his arm and plunged into the shed.

"Colin!" she called into the blackness. "What's in there?"

"Damn, it's dark in here," he yelled back. "This light isn't worth shit." Something metallic crashed over. "I think that was a bike." Another crash. "Two bikes."

He reappeared, cobwebs hanging from his hair, wheeling two rusty old bicycles. On one shoulder, a terrified spider perched after surviving the destruction of his home.

"Spider." Hannah pointed. Colin brushed it away and wrestled the bikes over the threshold and onto the grass.

"Jesus, these are ancient." The bikes were the upright kind, like something from the fifties. One rusty green and the other brown. The brown one also had a rotting wicker basket hanging limply from the front. As Hannah stood there, the basket suddenly broke from whatever tenuous strap had been holding it for the last sixty years or so and tumbled to the ground at her feet.

Colin and Hannah both looked at it, then at each other. "Hey, at least the tires have air," Hannah said. "Let's go for a bike ride."

Colin shrugged. "It's about time we took some pictures, right?"

∾

"Whoa." Hannah tried to steady the handlebars as her bike hit another rut, almost jolting her out of the seat. Her Pentax bounced on the strap slung diagonally across her chest. The front wheel wobbled. They'd turned off the road soon after leaving Pine House and for the last half hour had been bumping along on this overgrown footpath.

All around them, the piney woods clustered close. The only sounds were the constant rustling of the wind in the treetops, which kept making her think there was a waterfall somewhere nearby, and the occasional chirp of a cricket hidden in the thick carpet of pine needles that covered the forest floor. The woods stretched back and back, as far as Hannah could see. She shivered a little and pedaled faster toward Colin, who had dismounted from his bike up ahead and was replacing the rusty chain that had just fallen off for the fourth time. He grinned at her and stood up, wiping his greasy fingers on the back of his jeans. "My bike likes to test me," he said, throwing his leg over the seat again.

"Good thing you were a bike mechanic in another life." Hannah slowed and then followed as he took off once more, turning onto another path branching off to the right. This one was smooth with no ruts or weeds growing up the middle. It twisted and turned, winding through the forest like something out of a fairy tale. Hannah half expected to see Little Red Riding Hood appear, humming to herself and holding her basket for Grandma. The path turned sharply to the right and then left again. They dismounted at a small creek, almost dry, lifted their bikes over, and pedaled on. Numerous smaller paths branched off the larger path. Hannah began to feel disoriented. The woods looked the same—straight pine trunks, little spiny bushes everywhere, brown pine needles.

"Um, Colin?" Hannah called out. "Are we going to be able to find our way back? There's no markers or anything."

Her boyfriend's gray T-shirted back had already disappeared around the first bend. Hannah pedaled a little faster. "Colin!" she called again. The path was so twisty that she couldn't see more than a few feet of it at a time. He had to be just up there. "Colin!" she yelled louder. There was no answer.

A touch of anxiety made her stand up on her pedals, pumping harder, when suddenly, the front of her wheel slew sharply to the right. She felt herself toppling forward over the handlebars and that helpless, falling feeling—knowing you're going to hit the ground and that there's nothing you can do about it. The bike clattered to the ground at the same moment that her face hit the dirt, skidding a few inches. A sharp pain shot through her cheek and then everything came to a stop.

Hannah lay still a moment, smelling the musty old leaf smell on the ground, then pushed herself upright with her arms just as Colin pedaled back toward her. He threw his bike to the ground and knelt down beside her. "Han, are you okay?"

She sat up shakily. He looked at her face. "You have a huge scrape on your cheek." He reached out and touched it gently with the very tips of his fingers. "What happened?"

She lightly touched the abrasion that ran diagonally almost to her ear. "I don't know." Her voice still sounded a little trembly.

"I just slipped." She felt like crying, actually, but that would be ridiculous, crying over falling down and a scrape, like she was five.

"It's okay." Colin leaned in toward her. He gently kissed the scrape, his fingers massaging the back of her neck at the same time. "Hey, is your camera okay?"

She'd forgotten about it. They both looked around and found it lying forlornly on the ground a few feet away, like a little animal with its feet in the air. Hannah hoisted herself to her feet and went over to retrieve it. A smear of dirt on the case was the only sign of damage. She slung it over her neck and shoulder again and grabbed her bike, pulling it upright. Her face stung but she ignored the pain. "Okay, let's get going."

"Okay." Colin grinned at her and threw his leg over his bike too. Then he stopped suddenly. "Hey, look at that."

"What?" Hannah turned, following his pointing finger.

There, behind several layers of branches, was a small clearing of overgrown grass. The sunlight shone stronger through the trees and there was something else—a flash of something large, like a structure.

They slowly pushed their bikes over. The woods stopped abruptly at the clearing, as if a curtain of trees had been lifted. At the center stood a tiny church which must have been white at one point but which was more gray now. Its windows were boarded up and part of the roof sagged dangerously. Around the church, gravestones stood in roughly concentric circles. Even from a distance, Hannah could tell they were old ones—some lay tumbled on the grass, others were stained with long dark green streaks.

"What is this place doing back here?" She felt like she should whisper for some reason.

Colin raised his camera to his eye and clicked off a shot, then walked into the clearing. "There were probably other houses around at one point, something like that," he said. "Look at that one." He stopped and pointed to one of the graves, a large cross which had fallen over and was partly covered by tall grass, pinning it to the ground. "Dorcas Rejoyce," he read.

Hannah bent down, pulling aside the dry yellowing clumps, and inspected the barely-legible etching. "1805. Over two hundred years." She focused her camera on the grave. It looked different through the lens, removed, like a picture she was about to paint. Beside her, Colin's shutter clicked again and again as he photographed a worn granite angel on top of another grave. Just then something rang, faintly, like bells. Hannah looked around and, for one dream-like instant, thought that one of the graves was ringing. Then she realized it was only Colin's cell phone.

He dug the phone from his pocket as it rang once more, then stopped. Colin glanced at the screen.

"Who was it?"

"My mother. There's no service here though. Zero bars, but that's a good thing. Gives me an excuse not to talk to her." He thumbed the keypad rapidly and then stuffed the phone back in his jeans. "I just texted her that everything's fine. That'll keep her off my back for a few days."

"But there's no service. Will she even get it?" Hannah turned from Dorcas's grave and wandered toward the church.

"I don't know. No?" Colin laughed a little. "It'll go through once we're back at the house. There's some reception there."

Hannah knelt down and angled her camera upward, peering through the viewfinder. The church reared up against the overcast sky, gray against the whitish clouds. The boards on the windows stood out like wounds. Hannah lowered her camera and rose, looking around for Colin.

For an instant, she didn't see him among the gravestones, and her heart did a quick double jump. Then she spotted him, standing up on the steps of the church.

"Colin, what are you doing?" she called.

He was trying to peer through a small window to the right of the door, the only one unboarded. "Just checking things out," he said. He rattled the iron door latch, but it was locked tight.

Hannah glanced quickly through the dusty glass. She couldn't see much, just the looming shapes of some furniture draped with white sheets. Still, it was like looking through someone's bedroom window. She grabbed Colin's arm. "Come on. This place is giving me the creeps."

Colin rolled his eyes. "Worried the ghosts are going to get you?" he teased as Hannah hurried down the decaying steps.

"Yes, if you must know," she said over her shoulder.

Colin followed behind her but suddenly stopped. "Hey, cool," he said.

"What?" Hannah said impatiently.

He vaulted off the last few steps around to the far side of the church. Blueberry bushes grew thickly along the side of the old stone foundation there, basking in the heat of the western sun and clustered with so many of the bright, fat berries, they were almost sagging under the weight.

"Awesome," Hannah breathed. She climbed off the steps and plucked an experimental berry. It was soft and rich, hot from the sun. "Mmm," she said, busily plucking and eating.

Colin grinned at her. "I thought you wanted to leave."

Hannah couldn't help smiling back. "I do. After we get enough for a pie or something." For several minutes, they picked side-by-side in silence, the sun burning through the cloud cover, hot on their backs. The air was very still on this side of the church and scented with the rich, syrupy berry smell.

Then Hannah looked around, both hands full of berries. "I need a bucket."

Colin looked around also and then pulled his T-shirt off over his head. Quickly he tied a knot in one end, and held out the makeshift bag triumphantly.

"Nice." Hannah laughed, admiring the way the sunlight gleamed off his tan shoulders. The smooth muscles in his back rippled as he bent over the bushes once more.

Without thinking, Hannah leaned over, turning her head sideways, and laid her cheek down on his smooth back. His skin was hot from the sun and smelled deliciously of Irish Spring soap. Colin straightened up and turned around, wrapping his arms around her waist. Bending her backward, he pressed a long kiss against her throat. She could feel her pulse beating hard. The quiet forest noises around them—the rustling pine boughs and the occasional squawk of a robin from the trees—disappeared, and the world narrowed to a point as she focused entirely on the pressure of his cushiony lips against hers.

After a few minutes, Hannah straightened up, a trickle of sweat running down her side and into the waist of her shorts. She stood for a minute, heavy T-shirt bag in hand, looking out into the woods.

Colin put his hand on her back. He smiled at her a little and took her hand. "Come on. We've got plenty."

Hannah followed him around the side of the church, glancing behind her once as Colin led them back to the path and the bicycles. For a moment, she half expected to see someone standing there among the graves, someone like Dorcas, waiting for them, and her body tensed in anticipation. But there was no one, of course. Just the tall dry grass lying over in swathes and the quiet, patient gravestones.

They collected the bikes, and Colin tied the blueberry bag to his handlebars, where it swung heavily. The path continued past the church clearing, curving to the left and into the trees. Colin pointed. "You want to take that way back? It'll be more interesting than the main road."

Hannah wrinkled her forehead. "Are you sure that'll take us back?"

"Hannah, lighten up. It curves around. It probably meets up with the main path farther up. He started walking, pushing his clanking bike. "Come on," he called back over his shoulder. "Where's your sense of adventure?"

"My sense of adventure is fully intact," Hannah called after him, shoving her bike along. "Who was the one who thought to check out that old shed, anyway?"

They walked slowly down the path that wove like a stream through the tree trunks, following some unseen course of its own. This path was smaller than the one they'd taken on the way in, with roots lying in knotty lumps while branches reached down, gently scraping Hannah's scalp and lifting her hair as if with caressing fingers. Riding the bikes was impossible, so they walked on and on for what seemed like hours, but which Hannah knew was probably no more than thirty minutes.

Finally she stopped, leaning the bike against her legs, and flexed her aching wrists and arms. Rust flakes had rubbed off of the handles and were now sprinkled between her fingers. She wiped her palms on the back of her jeans. "Colin, I'm getting so tired," she called out.

He turned around. "Just a little farther, I think. The path might get wider up ahead and then we can ride."

"How much farther, do you think?" Hannah asked, squinting into the distance. Just more shadowy trees. Her watch said two o'clock, which meant they'd been walking for over an hour. It was hard to gauge the distance back since they'd been riding the bikes. And that made her a little nervous. *The Blair Witch Project* flashed into her mind. *Don't be stupid,* she argued with herself. *It just seems remote because you can't see far ahead. There're probably roads and houses all around here.* Her stomach gave a loud gurgle, distracting her momentarily from her ruminations. She pushed up next to Colin and dug into the T-shirt bag swinging from his handlebars, shoving a handful of plump blueberries into her mouth. She was beginning to wish she'd never let Colin convince her to take this way when suddenly, the trees grew thinner up ahead.

"Look, Colin!" she pointed. A band of gray had appeared beyond the trees, layered with the blue sky.

"Oh, nice," Colin said, walking a little faster. "I didn't know this would take us to the lake."

The path ended at another small, rocky beach, similar to the one in front of Pine House. They stepped onto the crunchy shingle and looked around. "There's the house," Hannah said. Pine House was about half a mile away, clearly visible against its dark green backdrop of trees. She could even see the blue towel she'd draped over the porch railing that morning after swimming.

"I don't think it'll take us too long to get back if we just follow the shoreline," she started to say before she realized that Colin was no longer standing by her side. "Colin?" She turned. The beach was empty. "Colin!" she called.

There was a crashing in the underbrush. Hannah whirled around in time to see Colin's bare back disappearing back into the woods.

"Colin! What are you doing?" she shouted. She sprinted after him, but he didn't stop. He was zigzagging around the trunks of the trees as he hurtled back down the path into the woods again.

Hannah's feet pounded on the hard-packed dirt. Her breath whistled in her ears. "Colin!" she shouted again. The beach was rapidly disappearing behind them, the path weaving into the darkness. Hannah forced her feet to run faster. A branch whipped her in the face.

Up ahead, she saw Colin stumble on a root. She closed the few feet in between them and grabbed his arm. She was shocked to find the muscles hard as a rock beneath her grasping hand.

"Colin, what are you doing?" she panted. He turned around slowly. A thrill ran through her when she saw his expression—it was blurred, dreamy, as if a sculptor had passed a hand over his face, half rubbing out his features.

He stared at her as if he couldn't remember who she was.

"Colin?" Hannah could hear her voice rise. He blinked, and the blurry look disappeared. His expression returned to normal.

Hannah dropped her hand slowly. Her heartbeat slowed. Colin looked around.

"Why'd you come back here, Han?" he asked. "I thought we were going home." He turned and started down the path again toward the beach.

Hannah stared at him. "Colin, what is the matter with you? *You* started running back down the path."

Colin's brow creased, as if he were concerned about her, and he placed his hand on her shoulder, rubbing it for a second before dropping his arm to his side. "Hey, we're both tired and hungry. I don't know why we're arguing. Let's just go home, okay?"

Hannah stared right into his familiar blue eyes. He looked back at her—his face as clear and sweet and open as always. "Okay," she said slowly. "That's probably a good idea." She swallowed and took his hand. It was ice-cold.

CHAPTER 13

The air in the bedroom was dampish when Hannah awoke from her nap later that afternoon. The window was gray, as if someone were pressing a sheet of metal against the pane, and the thick, rank smell of the lake hung in the room. Hannah shivered and, turning over, pressed herself more firmly against the warm, sleeping bulk of her boyfriend, groping around at the same time for her phone, lying beside her. She picked it up and squinted at the screen. Six o'clock. Jesus, they'd been asleep for almost two hours.

Hannah closed her eyes to see if she wanted to go back to sleep. But after a minute she opened them again. She was awake—might as well get up.

Colin was still sleeping peacefully, lying on his side with the blanket pulled up under his chin and his hands tucked under his cheek. On impulse, Hannah fumbled on the bedside table for her camera. She'd take a couple shots of him sleeping like that and show it to him later.

She bit back a giggle and groped around some more, then raised her head. On the bedside table were the drippy remains of a candle stub stuck in a saucer, a battered book of matches, and the stack of books, but no camera. She laid her head back onto the pillow with her hand on her forehead as she tried to remember where she'd put it. Where did she have it last? She squeezed her eyes shut, trying to remember. At the cemetery. She'd snapped those shots of the gravestones. And then she'd set it on the church steps to pick the blueberries . . . damn it! She'd left it on the steps.

She made herself take a deep breath. *Stop worrying. It'll be there later. It's not like someone's going to steal it out there in the woods.*

But it was so cloudy out. Hannah slid her legs out from under the warm covers and padded across the floor to peer out the little window. She could just see the edge of the lake and the side of the weedy lawn. The gray clouds hung heavily, so close to the lake that they seemed almost to touch it. Far away, Hannah thought she heard the rumble of distant thunder.

That was it. Quickly moving as quietly as she could, she stuffed her feet into her sneakers. Colin made a muffled noise and turned over on his back, his eyes still closed. He threw an arm over his head.

Hannah paused with her hand on the doorknob and looked back. His eyes were sweetly closed with his thick lashes lying in crescents on his cheeks. She could wake him. But no. She remembered how to get there. At a brisk walk, she'd be back in an hour.

Moving as silently as she could, Hannah cracked the door and slipped out into the shadowy hallway. She glanced at the cloudy sky and grabbed Colin's navy hooded sweatshirt from where it lay on the couch. All around her, Pine House lay quiet and still, like a sleeping dog. Hannah was tempted to remain, curl up on the couch with the big sweatshirt wrapped around her, and fall asleep for another couple hours.

Instead she forced herself to picture her Pentax sitting on the lonely church steps like a patient turtle. She turned resolutely and slammed out the door.

Outside, the mud smell seemed more pungent than ever. The thunder came again, closer this time, like a wolf growling and advancing.

Hannah hurried quickly around the side of the house. She hesitated as she passed the truck. Could she drive partway down to the main road to try to pick up the trail from there? No, she decided. She was safer retracing their steps. She pushed her way through the brambles that marked the trail, and started walking fast, swinging her arms purposefully, trying to ignore the faint sense of unease pressing at her back. Spiderwebs caught at her face and hair, and she brushed them aside with a little shudder. A branch cracked nearby. Hannah jumped and whipped her head around.

Just a raccoon or something. Stop freaking out. She took a deep breath and hurried a little faster. There was the little creek. It was higher now, the dark green water rushing over the almost submerged rocks. She tried to quell the growing sense that she never should have come into these woods by herself. What if she fell? What if she broke her leg? No one would know where she was. . . .

With her mouth set, Hannah balanced quickly across the creek and stepped onto the muddy far bank. Her sneakers slipped a little on the slick surface, and she reached out automatically, her hand grasping a wet branch, ruffly with lichen. The branch snapped in her hand and with a gasp, she pinwheeled her arms, trying not to fall backward into the water.

She caught herself and scrabbled up the bank, panting. *Made it. Okay, so calm down, Jesus, calm down. Nothing's out to get you, Han, okay?* The thunder rumbled again and a brisk breeze suddenly lifted her bangs from her sweaty forehead, sending the leaves rustling around her like a thousand whispers. The clouds grew darker, shutting out whatever dim light filtered down through the trees, as if it were already night.

Hannah hurried a little faster. *Okay, the turnoff, the turnoff. Find it fast, get the camera, and get home before the rain starts.* She scanned the trees lined up beside the path. They seemed practically identical, endless trunks and branches. The wind was blowing steadily now, keening high up in the treetops. Goosebumps rose on Hannah's arms.

Something caught at her hair, and she screamed, grabbing at her head. It was a branch, just a branch, tangled up in her hair. The turnoff. Had she passed it? Gone too far, too deep into the forest? A wave of vertigo swept her briefly. The pine trees seemed to shift suddenly, aligning themselves in rows and columns, as if generated on a computer. Hannah lifted her hand to her forehead, where a clammy film of sweat had broken out.

There it was. The opening—not ten feet away. She'd stumbled

past it. *Calm down.* She forced herself to take a deep breath, and the world straightened itself. She turned down the path and fifteen minutes later, the church came into view. The wind slackened as Hannah stepped into the clearing. The storm held its breath.

The camera was lying right where she'd left it on a corner of the church steps. The gravestones seemed to regard her solemnly as she wove through them, like eyes peering up from the ground. She looked down at Dorcas's grave. The grass she'd pulled up earlier now sat withered in a heap by its side.

Christ, this place was freaky. What the hell was the old church doing, just sitting in the middle of the woods like this? She pictured the dark interior inside, the rows of pews, the looming altar. The spirit of some old priest—someone who didn't like strangers poking around . . . *Stop it. You're being ridiculous.* Hannah kept her eyes fixed straight ahead. *Almost to the steps. Don't look up. Don't look at the church.* If she looked up, she might see the ghost of the old priest staring down from one of the windows, hand grasping the curtain, pulling it back—Hannah looked, her head drawn up as if against her will with her breath already caught in a half sob in her throat. Nothing. No one there. The boarded windows were dark and sightless as they'd been before.

Her heart pounding on unused adrenaline, she grabbed the camera from the steps and slung it around her neck. She forced herself to walk calmly but quickly away from the church.

Once in the safety of the trees, she slowed. Was this the path down to the beach? The second one. Or was it the third one?

The second one. It had that funny twisted branch hanging

down right in front of it. She walked faster, staring straight ahead. Just a few more minutes and she'd see the water. Follow the beach back to Pine House and slip into bed with Colin, all warm and sleeping.

The lake should be just ahead. Hannah strained her eyes but all she could see was more trees. Damn, these woods were deep. She felt like they would never end. A hairpin turn. No lake. Just more woods. *Okay, it's okay.* Her jaw ached, and she realized she was clenching her teeth. It's right ahead. You just can't see it yet.

She walked faster, then a little faster until she was almost running. The camera bounced against her rib cage. She rounded the next turn and stopped short.

A huge wall of rock stood directly in the center of the path. A boulder, actually, she realized after a second, but not one that had recently fallen. It had been there for a long, long time—long enough for thick ribbons of moss to climb up its sides and lichen to sprout in its crevices. The path ran right up to the boulder and then flowed around it like water.

She'd taken the wrong path—that was obvious. She took a deep breath, trying to ignore the band of panic tightening around her chest. Then the wind picked up, moaning through the trees in a disconcertingly human way. The light dimmed and the sky took on a yellowish cast. Hannah turned around. Go back. That was the only thing she could do. Go back and try to retrace her steps. Thunder suddenly boomed overhead. Hannah gasped. A small mewling sound escaped her throat. The sky was black, utterly black now. She heard the first fat raindrops hitting the dry needles all around her, as if a tiny army were approaching from all directions.

Fear welled up in Hannah's throat. She scurried beneath the thrashing branches. The wind rose to a shriek as it screamed through the trees and the rain fell faster, knife-sharp drops now that pierced Hannah's shoulders as if made of glass.

Thunder cracked overhead, an obscene sound, and with her breath coming in gasps, she began to run down the path. The trees flashed by. Her sneakers pounded the soil. *Get out, get out, get out*, her mind chanted like a mantra. The storm and the woods seemed like a huge malevolent entity, swirling around her—something that would not give up until it had her in its grasp.

She ran and ran but the path seemed endless. Damn it, she should be back by now, back to the turnoff by the church. Thunder cracked again and lightning lit the sky in violent blue-white streaks.

Then she heard it. Footsteps somewhere behind her, pounding the ground. Someone was back there. Following her. Someone else was in the woods. Hannah cast a glance back over her shoulder as she ran. Nothing—too dark. Footsteps. Crackling branches. She ran faster, hands outstretched. Her breath whistled in and out of her open mouth. The footsteps still came, closer now, pounding like hers. Whoever it was, they were running too. She slipped, her fingers meeting the muddy ground and scrambled up again and ran on.

Then from behind her someone was shouting. "Wait! Stop!" Fingers touched her back. Hannah turned and looked up into Colin's wide eyes. He was panting, his shirt only half-buttoned and his hair wet with rain. Rain glistened on his chest and arms. "Jesus, I was calling and calling you." He breathed heavily for a second, bracing his hands above his knees. "What were you doing, running away like that?"

Hannah blinked. All the color was returning to the world. For the first time, she realized her clothes were soaked through to the skin. Slowly she opened her mouth to answer but at that moment her knees buckled, and she would have fallen to the ground if Colin hadn't caught her by the arm.

"Careful there." He wrapped an arm around her shoulders. "You're a mess."

"I know," Hannah croaked. His arm felt very strong and warm. She leaned into his shoulder and let her eyes half close. The fear, the overwhelming fear that had propelled her from the church through the woods, drained away. There was only Colin now—solid and real. "You came to find me," she muttered as he steered them along the path.

"Hell yeah, I came to find you. I wake up to find my girl-friend gone and a huge storm going on outside, you think I'm just going to roll over and go back to sleep? Careful, root." He guided her to the right. Ahead only a few hundred feet was the road.

Hannah felt her muscles beginning to shake from the damp and exhaustion. "What's the road doing here?" she mumbled.

Colin rewrapped his arm around her more firmly. "It's always been here, babe. It doesn't move around."

"That's what you think," Hannah muttered.

"What?" Colin bent to hear her.

Hannah raised her head and forced her numb lips to articulate. "I came in on the other path, the one from earlier. I had to get my camera before it got rained on." She held up the sodden Pentax.

Colin nodded, his eyebrows raised. "I thought it might be something like that." The trees parted and the truck came into sight, parked crookedly at the side of the road. Hannah thought she'd never seen anything so beautiful. Colin steered her toward the passenger door. "Let's get you home."

Hannah groaned and hauled herself up into the seat, sinking down on the worn plush. Colin slammed the door on the driver's side and started the engine, backing around carefully until they were pointed back toward Pine House.

The rain had lessened to a steady shower, and the thunder had moved out of the area. The windshield wipers made a steady *shush-shush*, the headlights cutting two beams into the gray gloom outside. Hannah sat back in the seat, her eyes closed. Her bones seem to have dissolved, leaving her completely limp. *God, what a weird day. And Colin having that freak-out earlier. Were they having some sort of reaction to being alone? Like cabin fever?*

"So, do you want to tell me what you were doing, tearing through the woods like that, crying?" Colin's voice fell calmly on her ears.

Hannah forced her eyelids open. "I don't know. The church started freaking me out. I kept thinking someone was watching me. And then I went the wrong way to get back and I got scared, like I'd be lost forever, and then I thought someone was chasing me and I completely lost it. . . ." Her voice trailed off, and she let her head fall back on the seat again. "It was so weird. I don't think I've ever been so scared before."

"Someone *was* following you. Me." Colin stopped the car. Hannah looked around. They were in front of Pine House, which all of a sudden looked very cozy and welcoming with the door partially ajar and a candle burning in the front window where Colin had left it.

Hannah climbed shakily from the truck and walked slowly up the path. She felt like an old, old woman. All her muscles ached, as if someone had been beating her over with a bat. She mounted the steps and crossed the creaky porch. Colin shoved the door open silently. The living room was dim, lit only by the yellow flicker of the candle. Hannah collapsed onto the old couch and leaned her head back on the mashed yellow pillows. She closed her eyes. She felt like it was midnight.

She stared at the darkness behind her eyelids for what seemed like a long time until she felt the touch of wool on her bare, wet shoulders. She opened her eyes. Colin was bending over her, draping a striped blanket around her.

She gathered the folds around her shoulders and gazed up at his face, which was thrown into deep relief by the flickering candlelight. His hair was partially dry, like hers, and standing up in rough spikes. His blue eyes were crinkled with concern. He sat down next to her and put his arm around her shoulders, pulling her in close and rubbing her arm firmly.

Hannah sighed and leaned her head on his shoulder. He laid his head on top of hers. They were quiet for a long time. The only sound in the room was the light tapping of the steady rain against the big windows.

Hannah raised her head. "You saved me, you know."

Colin smiled down at her. He brushed a strand of damp hair from her forehead. "I did."

"You knew I was in trouble, and you came for me." She raised her head to look into his face.

He nodded, a little smile crimping his mouth.

Hannah opened her mouth. She felt the words building up in her throat. Her body was so tired, so warm and limp lying there under the blanket, that she didn't have the strength to resist. "I needed you." She couldn't remember ever having said those words before.

Colin blinked. "You did." He seemed to be waiting for something.

"I couldn't get home myself. I needed you." Her voice was growing stronger now.

Colin nodded slowly. "Yeah."

A tremulous feeling started in Hannah's belly. She sat up, throwing off the blanket and turned to face Colin. She took his hands and his long fingers closed immediately around hers.

His eyes searched hers. "Han, I've always been here. I think today is just the first time you've ever let me help you." He smiled suddenly. "Or maybe it's the first time you've needed help. Lucky me."

"No," Hannah whispered, holding onto his fingers very tightly. "Lucky me."

CHAPTER 14

"I don't think this pie is working out!" Hannah called into the depths of the house. She wiped the back of her hand on her perspiring forehead and gazed dolefully at the pile of cracker crumbs on the counter in front of her. Beside the crumbs sat the blueberries, now washed and ready for their transformation into blueberry pie. Using crushed-up saltines, dug from one of the cabinets, mixed with milk and water seemed like a good idea half an hour ago. But now they were stubbornly refusing to turn into any sort of crust. "And to make a blueberry pie you need a blueberry pie *crust*," Hannah mumbled to herself. "Otherwise you'll have blueberry sauce."

"And I want a blueberry pie, woman," Colin ordered, coming into the kitchen, damp from the shower, and catching the last portion of her mumbled soliloquy.

"Yeah, and then you can drag me around by my hair, is that right, Grog?" Hannah picked up the rolling pin for the eightieth time.

Colin came up behind her and wrapped his arms around her. "Mmm, barefoot and in the kitchen, that's how I like you," he said into her neck.

Hannah giggled and her skin tingled from the rush of his breath. "I like *you* barefoot and in the kitchen," she said, leaning back against him and stretching her arms back and around him. With dry clothes, a piece of bread with peanut butter in her stomach, and several candles placed around the kitchen, her terror in the woods seemed like it had happened years ago, instead of just a couple of hours.

Colin released her and wandered back into the living room. "Going outside for a sec," he called. The screen door slapped and his footsteps clattered on the back steps.

Hannah focused on the crumbs in front of her and read the recipe again. The cookbook page was yellowed and stained here and there with the long-ago smears of other fruit pies. She squinted at the page. "One peck of blueberries, mixed with the juice of one lemon and a pint of flour." A *peck* of blueberries? Was that a lot or a little? Did this thing have a glossary or something? Hannah wiped her hands on the rear of her jeans and flipped to the back of the book, then the front. Nothing, but the copyright was 1935. No wonder she didn't know what a peck was. This book must have been Colin's grandma's or something.

Hannah grabbed a glass pie plate from one of the open cupboards, dumped the blueberries into it, and scattered the saltine crumbs on top. There. It would just be an open-faced pie. Kind of like an open-faced sandwich.

She was examining the dials of the old white stove, trying to figure out how to turn on the oven, when the back door slapped again and Colin came in. His face was flushed. Hannah straightened up.

"What's up? You look kind of red." She noticed a sheen of sweat on his forehead. "And you're sweaty. Ew."

Colin set his camera down on the table. There were slick, wet finger marks on the black case. He blinked and touched his forehead. "Oh yeah. It's humid out. I think it's going to storm again." He peered over her shoulder. "Did you figure this out?"

"No." Hannah pointed at the dials. "I don't even know how to turn it on."

"How about this one?" He twisted one labeled ON/OFF. There was a clicking sound, then a muffled *flump* from back inside the oven. Colin straightened up and patted his chest. "Don't worry, you can thank me later."

"I will—with open-faced saltine pie." Hannah scraped the last of the crumbs from the cutting board and dumped them onto the pie.

Colin leaned back on the counter. "Saltine pie, is that what you're calling it?" He grinned wickedly. "Remember the first time you tried to make me dinner?"

Hannah winced. "Oh God. Flank steak and baked potatoes. Please don't remind me." She opened the oven door and put her hand inside. Hot. She slid the pie in. "In my own defense, can I just say that I was insanely nervous?"

Colin's grin widened. "The potatoes exploded all over the inside of the oven. And—"

"—the steak was still frozen. I remember. And we didn't know each other well enough to say anything, so we both just sat there, trying to eat it, pretending it was great." Hannah picked up a blue-striped dishcloth and hid behind it. "I can't believe you still wanted to go out with me after that."

Colin reached out and grasped one of Hannah's hands. "You know how I knew I wanted to go out with you again?" His voice was low and intense, but Hannah didn't want to look away. She kept her eyes fixed on his shining blue ones.

He went on. "That meal with you was the first time I can remember really talking to a girl who was actually listening."

Hannah squeezed his hand back. "I even remember you told me how you were a vegetarian for two days in fourth grade because you read *Charlotte's Web*." She looked down at their entwined hands. Suddenly she wanted nothing more than to be buried in the embrace of his arms. She stood up and tugged at his hand, pulling him into the living room, where she collapsed on the old couch. Reaching up, she pulled him down with her.

Colin fell on top of her, and, while giggling, she tried to shove him to the side. "I wanted you to cuddle with me—not squash me!" she gasped. Outside, the wind was picking up again, sighing through the treetops and then rising to a shriek. The glass in the windows rattled.

Colin raised his head, listening. "Another storm."

Hannah shivered as the light in the room grew darker, and Colin looked down at her.

"It's okay." He smoothed her hair and then encircled her with his arms. For a long moment, the world narrowed to a point filled only with his firm mouth on hers and the rush of his breath on her cheek.

Hannah closed her eyes. Colin's lips left hers and traveled down her neck to the base of her throat. A tingle shuddered down her spine.

He raised his head, gazing at her steadily, and something about the determined look on his face told her that he wasn't going to say it. He was going to wait for her. She thought this would upset her, but instead the words bubbled up to her lips, like water from a spring. She took a small breath. His eyes—calm and patient—fixed steadily on hers, holding her in place. Her lips parted. "Colin," she managed.

"Yeah?" His voice was almost a whisper

The words rose up in her throat, crowded her lips and teeth. "Colin, I—"

Her words were cut off by a massive crash from outside. The picture window rattled violently in its frame. Hannah screamed, bolting upright. Outside, the sky rolled black and angry. Through the window, Hannah could see towering gray thunderheads scudding in across the lake, where the pine trees now formed a jagged, forbidding barrier.

Suddenly lightning split the sky, striking the lake. The wind whipped the trees around the house, raining down twigs and small branches. Hannah must have let out a whimper because Colin placed a comforting hand on the back of her neck. "It's just a storm."

"I know. Are there tornadoes around here?" She tried to sound relaxed, but another clap of thunder shook the roof, followed immediately by a bolt of lightning. The storm was getting closer. On the windowsill, the lone candle sputtered in the holder, then died, leaving the room in darkness.

Hannah scooted closer to Colin, burying her head in his chest.

"Hey, come on, it's okay," he comforted her, stroking her hair. "At least we don't have to worry about the power going out."

"Ha-ha," Hannah mumbled into his chest.

Then thunder cracked and a massive purple-white flash filled the room. The air was suddenly full of electricity. Hannah could feel her skin prickling and for an instant thought that she'd been struck by the lightning. She shrieked and cowered against the couch cushions. "What was that?" she half screamed and half gasped. She pushed herself up and swiped her hair out of her eyes.

"I don't know." Colin was breathless too, sitting up and looking around. "I think lightning hit something really close."

"Like the house?" Hannah's voice rose with a touch of hysteria. "Is it on fire?"

"I don't know." Colin rose to his feet. Hannah could hardly hear him over the din of the rain pounding the tin roof. "Do you smell smoke?"

Hannah sniffed anxiously. "No . . . but there's some kind of draft." She hugged her arms. Cool, damp air rolled through the room, as if a door had been opened somewhere in the depths of the house.

Colin rose from the sofa. Hannah clutched at his hand. "Wait, don't leave me here!" The room flickered like a strobe as lightning flashed constantly. Hannah could hear the house creaking above the rush and rustle of the leaves.

Colin gripped her arm. "Come on. Something happened in there." He indicated the back of the house. The entrance to the hall was as black as an open throat, waiting to swallow them up. He lit a candle beside the couch and cupped his hand around the flame.

Hannah grasped the back of Colin's shirt as they crept down the long hallway. The door to the child's bedroom was open and flapping. The cold air curled around Hannah's ankles and brushed her face like trailing fingers.

Colin peeked through the doorway, a little at first, then all the way. He held the candle high. "Damn!" he exclaimed over the howl of the wind.

Hannah peered over his shoulder and gasped. In the dim light, she could see a huge tree branch, at least two feet in diameter, crashed through the window over the desk. Wet green leaves and twigs were all over the floor. The desk itself was overturned and the top almost split in two. Rainwater splattered the navy comforters on the twin beds pushed against either wall. Papers, pencils and little toys were hurled everywhere.

"Colin, look." Hannah pointed to the base of the branch, poking out of the window. Long black char marks ran vertically up the wood. The end of the branch was black as charcoal.

Colin inhaled. "Struck by lightning."

They stared at each other wide-eyed, and Hannah exhaled with a shaky laugh. "Can we go home now?"

They backed out of the room, and then Colin reached out and closed the door firmly. He steered Hannah down the hallway toward their bedroom. It was so dark that she could barely see her own feet.

The storm noise seemed quieter somehow in their room. Maybe because there was just the one small window. Hannah curled up in the middle of the bed as Colin struck a match and lit the bedside candle. He lay down beside her, and the yellow glow deepened the shadows of his face. Hannah yawned, her eyelids drooping. The soft old comforter seemed to envelop her in warmth. The storm had lessened and the rhythmic drumming of the rain was almost hypnotic now. She sighed and turned over, pressing her back against Colin.

"Han? The pie?" she heard him say, as if from a great distance.

She couldn't respond. Sleep was too close. Dimly, she felt him get out of bed and return a moment later.

"I took it out," he said. "Han? You know before, when we were laying on the couch . . . you were saying . . ."

But she never heard the rest of his words because sleep had risen up and pulled her down into velvety blackness.

CHAPTER 15

Hannah opened her eyes. At first she didn't know why she'd awakened. Then she heard it—a scratching sound coming from down the hall. She tensed, listening for a minute, but the sound didn't return. Hannah relaxed back onto the pillow, flinging her arm over to the other side of the bed. But instead of the sleeping body of her boyfriend, she hit only rumpled blankets. She raised her head. Colin was gone.

"Colin?" she whispered to the empty room. No answer. The silvery moonlight poured over the bed, but the dresser was only a dark bulk in the corner. The door to the hall stood partly open.

Hannah swung her feet over the edge of the bed and then paused. The house was utterly still. Maybe Colin was just in the bathroom. She strained her ears for the sound of the toilet flushing or water running or anything.

Nothing. Outside the window, she could hear the pine trees talking softly to themselves in the night breeze. Faintly, eerily, the laughing call of a loon rose from the lake. Hannah shivered. She forced herself to lie back down and pulled the sheet up around her shoulders. Colin was . . . out by the car? Maybe he was getting something?

At three o'clock in the morning, Hannah?

She fumbled for the matches and, lighting the bedside candle, climbed out of bed and padded to the door, clad only in Colin's LEXINGTON 5K T-shirt and her underwear. "Colin?" she called out into the hallway. No answer.

"Colin!" she said again, louder. The air in the rest of the house was cool and fresh. It still smelled vaguely of damp leaves. Hannah was about to dart back into the bedroom for her sweatpants when she heard the scratching sound again. "Colin? Is that you?" she called, going toward the scratching. Dumb question, of course. Who else would it be?

The door to the child's room was partially closed. Hannah could see the edge of Colin's foot as she approached, holding the dripping candle high. "Hey, what are you doing? It's freezing in here," she said as she pushed open the door.

Colin was kneeling on the mud-smeared floor in front of the broken desk, wearing khaki shorts but no shirt. A candle burned on the floor beside him. The tree limb poked through the broken window, its leaves still green, but now hanging dispiritedly from the branches. Colin held a handful of rumpled, rain-spotted papers in his hand. He looked up at the sound of her voice and Hannah recoiled, staggering back a few steps until she hit the door frame, which she grasped for support.

Her boyfriend's face was utterly slack, as if all the muscle tone had gone out of it. His mouth hung open a little, drool collecting in the basin of his bottom lip. His eyes were empty, as if he'd gone blind. But what was scariest of all was the utter lack of expression, the perfect blankness, as if someone had passed his hand over Colin's face, erasing it and leaving only eyes, a nose, and a mouth.

Hannah gasped, feeling the blood draining from her face. Her hands went cold. Involuntarily, she took another step back. Her foot hit something hard. A coffee cup rolled a few inches across the floor. It must have been lying there awhile because a damp brown splotch had already settled into the floor, partly staining the old blue rug.

"Colin?" she whispered.

He stared at her—through her—as if she weren't there. A little thread of saliva dangled from his bottom lip.

"Colin!" She started toward him, her mind already spinning. *Was he sick? Did he get bitten by some animal?*

Hannah knelt at his side. He remained still, his gaze directed toward the door, as if she were still standing there. She shook his shoulder. "What's the matter with you?"

Was he sleepwalking? She snapped her fingers in front of his eyes. Slowly, like a broken marionette, his head swung around. His eyes, two damp smears of blue, looked in her direction. But he wasn't focusing on her.

"Colin, what's wrong with you?" She had to restrain herself from screaming the words. Suddenly the old warning never to wake a sleepwalker flashed through her mind. They could have a heart attack or go insane, her mom always said. Oh my God, and she was trying to wake him up. Horror made her hands tingle. Shakily, carefully, she rose to her feet. Colin seemed not to notice her movements. He remained in the same position, kneeling on the floor in front of the papers, his head turned, staring at the opposite wall.

Carefully, she backed away. Her breath was coming in little hitches. She reached the doorway, trying to get a grasp on her racing thoughts. Okay, he was sleepwalking and that was definitely creepy, but she'd just go back to bed and when she woke up, he'd be awake too. Everything would be fine then, and they'd laugh about all this.

"Where are you going?"

She jumped at the sound of his voice. It was pitched almost an octave deeper than his usual voice. The words were slow, deliberate. Hannah stared at Colin, her mouth dry. She licked her lips. Were you supposed to talk to sleepwalkers?

"Nowhere," she whispered finally.

He gave no sign he'd heard her.

Hannah turned and fled down the hall, her feet pattering on the rough boards. She flew into the bedroom and collapsed on the edge of the unmade bed. Was he coming after her? Her eyes were wide and fixed on the empty doorway.

From down the hall, the floorboards creaked. Involuntarily, Hannah's muscles tensed. Her fingers gripped the bedsheets, slowly clawing them into a ball. Footsteps in the hall, slow and irregular, as if Colin was weaving back and forth as he walked. The footsteps approached, then stopped, then started again, but this time growing fainter, as if Colin were walking away.

Hannah sat on the bed for a long time, straining her ears for any sound from the house. But there was nothing. There was no clock in the room, so she tried to estimate how long since she'd last heard his footsteps. Fifteen minutes? Twenty? Her feet were growing cold and in spite of her tension, she began to feel sleepy again.

Then she heard him coming down the hall, faster this time. Without thinking, Hannah slid under the sheets and pulled the blankets up just as Colin entered the room. She squeezed her eyes shut and feigned sleep, drawing slow regular breaths. She forced her hands to relax on the mattress.

She heard him come closer. Hannah waited to feel the bulk of his body pressing down the mattress beside her. But instead the footsteps just stopped. She kept her eyes closed. He smelled like lake mud and leaves.

There was silence. Hannah willed herself to keep her eyes closed. She couldn't tell where he was. Then she heard the shift of cloth against cloth. He was standing by the bed. She had the strong sense he was watching her. A long moment stretched out. Then another. Still, he didn't move.

Hannah opened her eyes slowly, as if she was just waking up. Colin was standing over her next to the bed, staring down at her. The moonlight showed the smears of dirt on his bare chest and shorts. His face was dark and intense. The skin on the back of

Hannah's neck crawled. "Colin?" she whispered. "Where were you?"

"What are you doing in here?" His voice was harsh.

Hannah's stomach contracted. "What?" she whispered. "I'm sleeping."

He didn't seem to hear her. "Get up, Buggy." He pulled the covers back roughly. Hannah's breath caught as the cool air hit her skin.

"Who's Buggy?" Her voice rose. "You've never called me that before. Colin, are you still sleepwalking?" The words were out of her mouth before she realized what she was saying. If he was sleepwalking again, she shouldn't argue with him.

Carefully watching him, Hannah eased her legs over the side of the bed. "Okay, I'm up," she said.

This answer seemed to satisfy him, and he turned and walked back toward the door. Clutching her pillow, Hannah trailed a safe distance behind. For a sleepwalker, he seemed to know exactly where he was going. He walked straight down the hall and turned back into the child's room. Hannah followed.

Broken glass and splinters of wood lay all over the floor. Colin didn't seem to care, even though his feet were bare and caked with mud. He walked straight to the bed against the far wall, pulled back the navy blue spread and climbed in. He turned his face to the wall and was still.

Hannah stood alone in the middle of the floor for a long time, the damp night air pouring through the broken window and creeping up her legs. Maybe she should lie down in the other bed. It seemed like that's what he was indicating. She turned back the spread on the other bed, and laying her pillow on top of the other, slid between the cold, musty-smelling sheets. *This was just a weird episode. This is Colin. Your boyfriend. He's not even going to remember this in the morning. Go to sleep, and when you wake up, everything will be back to normal.* But even with these comforting thoughts rattling around her mind, it was a long time before Hannah could fall back asleep.

CHAPTER 16

Her phone was ringing at the bottom of the lake. She could see it, a hundred feet down in the murky water, the little screen glowing like a jewel. She treaded water as it rang and rang, and she had to answer because it was Colin calling. Colin needed her help. Hannah dove deep, kicking as hard as she could, eyes fixed on the little blue screen, while the water pressed at her mouth and chest and played with her long hair. Kick harder, pull harder, her mind instructed, get it before Colin hangs up, before he disappears. But she couldn't, it was too far and now the water was pressing even more insistently on her face, willing her to open her mouth as her lungs burned and screamed for air. She couldn't do it, couldn't make it, and she opened her mouth once and for all—

She jolted awake suddenly. The window was in the wrong place, she thought, disoriented, before remembering what happened the night before. Across the room, Colin was an immovable hump under the blue blanket. In the living room, her cell phone was trilling over and over.

Silently, Hannah slipped from between the covers and scurried out to the living room. She grabbed the phone and cradled it to her chest before tiptoeing out onto the front porch. She glanced at the screen. Laurie. She clicked the phone open.

"Hey," she whispered. "Hang on, okay?" She stepped off the front steps and crossed the yard to the edge of the woods, well away from the house.

"Okay, I'm here," she said in a normal voice, leaning back against a big jack pine.

"How's it going?"

"Are you at work?" Hannah eyed the house. All was still.

"Yeah," her friend replied. "The guys are on break." Her voice sounded echo-y.

"You sound like you're at the bottom of a bucket."

"Probably because I'm down here at the loading dock. The chemistry library is officially moved." Laurie sighed. "So, come on, I need a mental escape. Are you having the ultimate romantic weekend? Have I told you how insanely jealous I am?"

Hannah laughed nervously. "Yeah . . . you have." She paused a minute, wondering just how much to reveal. "Um . . . actually, things aren't going that well."

"What? What happened? Oh my God." Laurie caught her breath. "You guys didn't break up, did you? What happened?"

"No! Stop, nothing like that." Hannah twisted around and started picking a big piece of bark off the tree. The mosquitoes had found her. One buzzed drill-like near her ear. "I got lost in the woods yesterday and he came and rescued me and afterward, we were sitting on the couch, and I was really feeling like everything was right." The words tumbled fast from her mouth. "Like I could see he could take care of me, and I thought that this might be the moment to tell him I loved him. It just felt so easy to say it all of a sudden, but before I could, this huge storm blew up and—" Hannah stopped abruptly, breathless. On the other end, Laurie waited.

"And then last night, Colin was having some . . . um, sleeping problems." She could tell how weird that sounded as soon as the words were out of her mouth.

"*Sleeping* problems? What, was he snoring?"

"No, sleepwalking." Hannah suddenly wished she'd never started talking about it. Just hearing the words aloud made the whole situation seem even more real. "It's just—well, there was a storm, like I said," she went on, reluctantly. "And a branch crashed through one of the windows and then later, I found him staring at a bunch of these old papers, and he started calling me 'Buggy,' and then he made us sleep in a different room—"

"Okay, calm down," her friend soothed. "Just chill. Look, have you talked to him yet?"

Hannah took a deep breath and switched the phone to her other hand. She wiped her sweaty palm on the back of her leg. "Not yet. He's still sleeping."

"Well, just remember whom you're dealing with here—your *boyfriend*," Laurie went on.

"Right." Hannah could feel her heart starting to slow. Laurie's calm, ordinary voice spread like a balm over her jangled nerves.

"So, he's having some kind of sleep problem. Maybe he's stressed about leaving for Pratt. Maybe he's stressed about leaving *you*. Whatever. Just have a good time and you'll deal with it when you guys get back."

"Yeah . . ." Hannah said slowly. She willed herself to believe what her friend was saying.

"You're getting totally worked up over nothing." Laurie's voice grew tinnier.

"Are you walking? You're fading out."

"Yeah, the truck's here, so I've got to go. But look, stop freaking and just have fun with your boy. This is the last time you two will have for awhile."

"Yeah, okay," Hannah mumbled. She felt almost calm now. "Bye." She clicked the phone closed and stared over at the house. Everything was still. Only Pine House was watching her, big windows gazing back at her silently.

The rising sun was sending brilliant rays of pink and gold through the trees, but by some trick of the light, the surface of the lake was as opaque as a sheet of metal. Hannah thought of her dream, of diving deep down in that heavy water, and she shivered.

Stop. Stop it. She had to go inside anyway. The mosquitoes were attacking with a vengeance now. Hannah threw down the piece of bark she'd been twiddling in her fingers and started back toward the house. Laurie was right. She needed to stop freaking out. Colin was just having trouble sleeping. He *was* probably stressed out about Pratt. She didn't know why she hadn't thought of that before. Maybe when they got back, he'd go get something from the doctor. Ambien or something.

Holding this thought firmly in the front of her mind, Hannah mounted the porch steps. What she really needed now was some breakfast. Eggs and toast. They could do the toast over the gas flame on a fork. And maybe some of that jelly she'd seen shoved to the back of one of the cabinets.

In the kitchen, she lifted a cast-iron frying pan from its hook on the wall and gingerly lit the flame on the front burner, then cracked in four eggs from the bowl on the counter. The early morning sun streamed through the window at her back, throwing flickering shadows onto the stove and pan. She stirred the thick, lemon-colored yolks until they broke and blended with the clear white. Behind her, the silence of the house spread like water. She could feel it pressing at her back.

Snap out of it, Hannah. Everything was going to be fine. It was all perfectly normal—there had been a storm, and that branch had come through the window. And then it was just a coincidence that Colin had that bout of sleepwalking. But really, it could happen to anyone. Hadn't it happened to David sometime last year? Hannah scraped the pan more firmly with the old spoon.

The floor creaked behind her. "What are you doing?" Colin said.

Hannah whirled around. He stood in the doorway, wearing a T-shirt over his shorts now, his hair matted to one side of his head. The mud on his feet was dry, flaking off on the floor. But his eyes at least looked awake.

148

"Making eggs," she said, gesturing at the frying pan.

There was a silence, so still Hannah could hear a chickadee chirping outside on the porch.

"You know I hate eggs," Colin finally said softly.

Hannah blinked. "You do?" She paused. "We had eggs yesterday, though."

"I don't remember that." His voice was soft but cold, as if he was containing an explosion. "We always have oatmeal."

Hannah stared at him and swallowed. She heard the audible click in her throat. "Okay, um, what's going on? You're acting really weird. We've never had oatmeal."

He didn't even blink, just raised one eyebrow coolly. "I don't know what you're talking about. Are you lying again?" He turned and stalked into the living room. "Just make the goddamn oatmeal, will you?" he shot back over his shoulder.

Hannah stood frozen by the stove, the eggy spoon still in one hand. Her throat was tight. He'd never, ever sworn at her before. Never even raised his voice. She could feel tears building in her eyes. Was this some remnant from his sleepwalking?

The slap of the screen door started her out of her daze. She laid the spoon down on the stove and crossed into the living room. The back door was open.

She shoved open the screen. Colin was standing down on the beach, at the side of the lake. Feet scrunching on the gravel, Hannah pushed through the dank brown reeds. Her feet sunk into the mud as a rotted-fish smell rose up around her. Colin was leaning over the old rowboat, both hands on the edge, staring over the side into the empty interior.

"Colin . . . ," she started. Her voice shook, and she steadied it. "What is going on?"

Colin turned around. His eyes were wide and clear. "What do you mean?" He sounded genuinely puzzled.

"Do you remember anything that happened last night?" Hannah asked.

He shook his head. "What happened?"

Hannah threw her hands out at her sides. "You were acting completely bizarre, like you were sleepwalking. You were staggering around with this blank stare; you went outside; you made us sleep in the other room. Didn't you wonder where you were when you woke up this morning?"

Colin's eyebrows knit in confusion. "I was in our bed this morning, same as always."

"Colin, you weren't—" Hannah started to say and then stopped. Maybe he'd sleepwalked back to their bedroom after she'd left.

"And just now, in the kitchen," she went on. "You're acting totally mean. Why are you getting so mad about nothing?"

Colin just stared at her. Then he reached out and patted her shoulder. "Han, honestly, I don't know what you're talking about. Are you sure it wasn't *you* sleepwalking last night?" He turned, his sneakers making a sucking sound in the mud, and pushed past her, heading back toward Pine House. "Isn't it a nice morning?"

"Why were you accusing me of lying?" Hannah hurried after him, stumbling on the loose, smooth rocks that littered the dank sand of the beach. "I thought you liked eggs." She reached for his hand but he was already mounting the steps.

He turned around on the top step. His blue eyes perfectly matched the blue of the sky above him. "Han, I don't know what you're talking about." His face creased with concern. He reached out and touched her cheek. "You look tired."

"What—," Hannah spluttered, but just then her cell rang inside the house. She threw Colin one last despairing look and pushed past him into the living room.

It was her mom. Hannah grabbed the phone, her mind buzzing, trying to mentally prepare herself for the conversation ahead. She took a deep breath, steadied her hands and reminded herself that she'd been working at a job with Laurie this whole time—working very hard. She flipped open the phone.

"Hi, Mom." Her voice sounded surprisingly steady.

"Do you realize I've been trying you since last night?" Her mother's voice shrilled in her ear. "The call wouldn't go through."

Colin was crashing around in the kitchen now. Hannah cupped a hand over the phone and moved down the hall toward the bedrooms. "I'm sorry, Mom. You shouldn't worry. I told you the cell reception is really spotty here." There was a pause. Hannah could hear people talking faintly in the background, punctuated by the occasional ring of a cash register. "Are you at work?"

"Yes. Denise called in, so I'm covering for her." Her mother took a drink of something, probably her coffee.

"Oh, Mom, a double shift?" Hannah sank down on the edge

of the unmade bed. A ball of guilt sank into the pit of her stomach. "Who's taking care of David?"

Her mother sighed. "Mrs. Robinson again. I told her I'd pay her extra since I'm not going to be back until so late."

"Mom, I'm really sorry. . . ." Hannah paused, twirling the sheet around her finger.

"For what?" Her mother was walking now. "You're working hard, making triple time—that's such a help, Han."

Hannah swallowed. "Yeah," she whispered.

"So how's it going up there? Laurie's dad's not working you too hard, is he?"

Before Hannah could answer, there was a flurry of voices in the background. Hannah's mom came back on the line. "I've got to go, baby. They want me at the register. Be good, work hard, okay?" She made a kissing noise into the phone.

"Okay." Hannah kissed back, and then her mom was gone.

Slowly, she flipped the phone closed. Out in the kitchen, Colin was still banging pots around and singing snatches of "Country Road," by John Denver.

She stood up and for lack of anything better to do, flipped the blankets back to make the bed. The top sheet pulled out from where it had been tucked under the mattress and several sheets of paper fluttered to the floor. Hannah stared at them a moment, then picked them up. They were the papers Colin had been looking at in the night. One was a newspaper clipping. "Franz's Garden Store," read a full-page ad on one side. "Zinnias, all shapes, all colors." Hannah flipped the clipping over.

"Breakfast!" Colin's footsteps came down the hall. Hannah gasped and shoved the papers under the mattress again, standing up just as her boyfriend appeared in the doorway, holding a saucepan of something. "Breakfast," he said again, holding the pan out like an offering. "I made oatmeal. Your favorite."

Hannah stared at him. "Right," she said slowly and followed him back down the hall.

They ate quickly, in silence, hunched over their bowls. Colin shoveled the last bite of oatmeal into his mouth and laid down his spoon. He smiled at her and Hannah smiled back, her heart suddenly rising.

"You want to go swimming?" he asked.

Hannah blinked. "Um, I thought you weren't really into it. Remember you told me about that yesterday?"

He just gazed over her shoulder. "Okay, let's go," he said, as if she'd given a different response entirely. He rose from his chair and brushed past her. Hannah remained frozen at the table. At the back door, Colin paused, seeming to realize she wasn't following him, and turned around slowly.

Hannah's heart gave a single huge thud. His eyes were clouded again, dreamy, as they'd been last night. Christ, was he sleepwalking *now*? No, that's impossible. He was awake—he *is* awake. Hannah licked her lips, which suddenly seemed very dry.

"Come on," Colin said deliberately. He pushed out the door.

Hannah tiptoed across the floor and watched as he crossed the sand to the edge of the water. She expected him to strip down and plunge into the water, but instead, he gazed out across the lake to the edge of the woods where they had emerged from the church the other day.

Then he turned sharply to his right and walked a few feet over to the rowboat slung drunkenly among the reeds. He stood perfectly still staring at the rowboat for a long time. Then he returned to his spot by the water, pulling his shirt over his head. Hannah gripped the windowsill with both hands. Oh my God, was he going crazy? Was he on drugs or something? No, no way. Colin would never do something like that. And he wasn't acting drunk, not at all. Maybe she could slip back inside, hide out in one of the bedrooms, just until he got over whatever this was. And the minute they got back home, she'd make him see a doctor.

But before she could move, Colin called out, "Come on, babe," without turning around.

Slowly, Hannah pushed open the screen and went down the steps to the lake's edge. Colin turned as she reached his side. He smiled at her, his own smile. It was gentle and open. Hannah felt herself relax. Okay. So he was having some trouble, and he was definitely acting strange. But he was still her own Colin. She needed to remember that.

Hannah stripped down to her underwear, and Colin took her hand and started walking into the water, still wearing his shorts. He didn't seem nervous at all now. Instead, he walked stolidly forward, towing her by the hand like a package, until the water was chest high. Then he released her and began swimming around in a circle, his hair dark with water and shiny as a seal's.

Hannah watched him carefully. His face was expressionless. She debated whether to ask him again if he was okay, or maybe if he was taking something. But no. Better not upset him. Just wait for now.

Hannah stared down into the thick green murk. Her arms disappeared at the elbow when she sliced through the water, as if she were amputating them over and over. She thought of her dream—of what it would be like to dive deep down into that darkness, into the weeds and mud at the bottom.

As she came nearer, Colin suddenly turned and in one movement, scooped her into his arms. "This is fun, isn't it?" His skin was chilly and covered with goose bumps. He looked pale and the shape of his face was strange with his hair plastered to his forehead. In the slanting sunlight, it looked brown instead of blond and his eyes looked dark too. Almost like he was a different person.

"Yeah, fun," she managed to say. Gently, she tried to extricate herself from his grasp, but his arms tightened like two steel bands around her.

"I always love it when we swim together," he said, still in that husky voice. His arms slipped from her shoulders down to her waist as he pulled her in closer to him.

Hannah gasped a little. "You're squeezing me hard," she said, struggling. She forced a little laugh. "And, we only swam together the one time—yesterday, remember?"

"Oh yeah," Colin said. His voice was distant. He dropped

his head to her shoulders and let his cold lips trail along her collarbone. "I remember perfectly."

Hannah shivered at the touch in spite of herself. She didn't believe him.

CHAPTER 17

She was running through the woods again, clutching Colin's camera, panting, hair streaming. The sky was black with twisting clouds, and the tree trunks flashing in front of her had grown to freakish proportions, creaking, leaning onto the path, reaching out to snag her as she stumbled past, her breath sobbing in and out of her throat. Behind her, someone was coming. Footsteps were pounding on the dirt path. The terror rose up in her throat, choking her. Whoever it was, he was coming for her.

Hannah shook her head and blinked hard, trying to focus again on the black print that swam in front of her vision. She rubbed her forehead. After swimming, Colin had lain down on the living room couch and immediately fallen asleep, and she'd wandered out to the porch with a stack of old magazines to think things over quietly. But her mind kept wandering to places she'd really rather not go.

The day had turned gray and humid, the air hanging like a

EMMA CARLSON BERNE

wet rag, sullen and heavy with the dank smell of the lake mud. The windows of the house were silver with moisture. Hannah looked down at the pages of *Quilting Today* magazine in her lap. Something was wrong with Colin, and she didn't know what to do. They had to just go home. Today, she resolved, staring at the magazine page. "Bird-in-the-Window patterns are perfect for the beginner!" the headline chortled. The screen door slammed behind her, and Hannah stiffened.

"Hi."

She twisted around. He was smiling, a coffee cup in his hand. His hair was tousled charmingly. He looked like her old Colin again.

Relief flooded Hannah's heart. She had to restrain herself from leaping off the step and hugging him. "Hi," she managed tremulously.

He came over and dropped a kiss on top of her head, then set his coffee cup down on one of the porch posts. "Nice day." He looked around appreciatively, inhaling. Sullen thunder rumbled in the far distance.

"Um, yeah," Hannah tentatively agreed. "It's getting kind of hot."

"I love that breeze through the pines," Colin replied. He went over to the shed where they'd extracted the bikes and opened the door.

Hannah looked around at the still trees and utterly flat lake. Even the leaves on the oaks hung limp.

Colin returned from the shed lugging a heavy wooden toolbox.

158

He walked purposefully over to the truck, which sat at the corner of the overgrown yard, and reaching inside, popped the hood.

"What're you doing?" Hannah asked.

He propped the hood open and poked his head inside. "Got to take care of that clanking noise," he said, his voice partially muffled by the hood. He bent down and selected a wrench.

Hannah blinked and laid her magazine to one side. "What clanking noise?" she called across the yard. "I don't remember it clanking."

Colin stuck the wrench into the engine and twisted something. He didn't even look up. "The engine's about to go, believe me. I heard it the other day." He dropped the wrench and picked up a pair of pliers. "Damn, this relay is on tight." He gripped the pliers more tightly and jammed them into the engine hard. Hannah winced. She laid her magazine aside and crossed the yard.

Colin was tugging on something deep in the engine. "Little fucker is completely stuck," he growled. Hannah had never heard him say "little fucker" in her entire life. She took a deep breath. *This is your boyfriend who loves you,* she reminded herself. *He's just having some problems. Talk to him—just tell him what's on your mind.*

"Colin, listen," she said. He didn't look up. He was gripping a gray boxy thing with the pliers, yanking at it. "Um, maybe we should think about heading out." She gripped the edge of the truck hood. The metal was hot, almost scorching the pads of her fingers.

Colin looked up. His hair tumbled over his forehead, and

there was a smear of grease on his cheek. "What're you talking about? Are you leaving me?" His forehead creased with distress.

Hannah shook her head, squeezing the hood tighter. "No, no, Colin. Listen . . . I, um, I think it's time to go. I mean, we've had a really good time here, but my mom's probably wondering how much longer this job with Laurie is going to last. And . . ." She took a deep breath. "Things have seemed weird since last night. I'm kind of worried." She looked up at last into his face, not sure what she would find there.

Colin stared at her, the wrench still clenched in one hand. "Sure, babe, we can leave whenever you want," he said. "We can leave tomorrow morning—how's that? Run away and never come back?" He grinned at her.

"Yeah . . ." Hannah said slowly. "Tomorrow morning's great." Something didn't feel right, but she couldn't quite put her finger on it. He'd agreed to leave after all. That was good.

Colin nodded in an abstracted way and turned back to the engine. He pulled harder. "Ah! Got it. We'll be all right now." He grinned at her.

Hannah watched him for a second longer, then trailed back across the yard and into the house. In the kitchen, she sank down at the old wooden table and rested her head on her hands. She'd done it, she thought, staring between her elbows. She'd said what she was worried about and he'd agreed they could leave tomorrow.

Hannah traced a circle on the table with one finger. This was supposed to be their big trip, and it hadn't turned out at all like she thought. She pictured the branch still stuck in the other room. The stagnant, silent lake. Colin outside, poking at the truck with his wrench. Everything had gone wrong since last night, and now they were going to go off and leave—the end of their trip just fizzling out.

What if she did something about it though? Hannah sat up and then pushed her chair back. What if they had a picnic tonight, out on the beach? Maybe a special occasion would snap him out of his daze.

Hannah jumped up and began pulling open all the cabinets and drawers. There wasn't much food left—some cherries, three peaches, a handful of the blueberries from earlier. A jar of olives. Some almonds in a bag they'd brought in from the truck. There was a quarter loaf of bread and a hunk of cheese. Not much, but if she put it all in little bowls, it would seem like a picnic. They could spread out a blanket, watch the sun set, feed each other olives, say their last good-byes to Pine House. Hannah could feel her spirits slowly rising. Maybe they could salvage the end of the trip. Maybe Colin would snap out of his daze. Maybe whatever had been carried in on that storm would float away on the evening breeze and things could just go back to the way they were before.

CHAPTER 18

The evening couldn't be more perfect, Hannah thought later that night, as she leaned back on the blanket and stretched her feet out toward the water. Across from her, Colin popped an olive into his mouth and smiled. Fixing the truck must have relaxed him. He looked almost like his old self, just like she'd hoped. Hannah lifted her face to the night breeze. The humidity of the day had blown away as the sun set, and now the air was fresh with the faintest hint of a chill, as if autumn was coming two months early. Colin would be leaving so soon. A melancholy pang struck Hannah's throat. She reached out across the blanket and took his hand. "What am I going to do senior year without you?" she said.

Colin shook his head. "I don't know," he said. "Suffer?" He grinned.

Hannah laughed—the first time she'd laughed since the storm, she realized. "I will," she said. "You want some cherries?" She extended the bowl toward Colin.

"Sure." He reached over and grabbed a dark red one. "Come here." He extended the cherry toward her, and she leaned over obligingly and opened her mouth, biting down and squirting red cherry juice on his white T-shirt.

"Hey!" Colin laughed, brushing at himself. "Direct hit."

"It looks like you've murdered someone." Hannah laughed and stretched on her back on the blanket, staring up at the night sky, black now, and studded with thousands of diamond-bright stars. He seemed fine. Maybe the spell was broken. Maybe whatever was wrong with him was just like a bad dream that was over. She'd woken up and the old Colin was back.

Hannah wriggled over until she collided with her boyfriend on the other side of the blanket. He was stretched out on his back also, and she rolled on top of him so they were lying face to face. He smiled, his eyes closed, and put his arms around her. She studied his beautiful, familiar face, tracing his golden eyebrows with the tip of her fingers. "Colin," she said softly.

He smiled, his eyes still closed and pulled her closer. "Hmm," he said.

"I'll really miss you." She leaned down and pressed her lips to his. "I—" She choked on the words, fighting with herself. This had to be it. There weren't that many moments left until he went away. But it was hard to get the words out. It was so revealing. It made her so vulnerable. Hannah jumped up abruptly, walking to the edge of the water.

Behind her, she could tell Colin was watching her, waiting. She glanced around for some sort of distraction, anything. Her eye fell on the rowboat drawn up a few yards away. On impulse, she went over to it, her feet crushing the reeds beneath, and peered inside where the two oars lay across the bottom.

"Hey, we should take this thing out. I can't believe we've been here all this time and never gone for a row." She moved around to the back and gave the boat an experimental push, to see if it would move out from the shore. To her surprise, it moved almost immediately, instead of being mired in a decade's worth of mud like she expected.

"Check this out!" Hannah called.

Colin was sitting on the blanket, but she couldn't see him very well. His form was just a dark bulk on the sand. He said something she didn't catch.

"What?" She could see him stand up and move toward her.

"I said I hate boats." His voice sounded strained.

Hannah gave the boat another push and waded a foot or so into the water. The boat was floating now. "You hate boats, you hate swimming. What's the deal with you and water, Colin?"

He was walking toward her more rapidly now.

"Stop it, Hannah," he said. His voice was strained. "Don't touch it."

A feeling of rebellion rose up in Hannah's chest. Her face grew unexpectedly hot. "You know, Colin, you've been acting really strange all day," she said, still leaning down with both hands on the boat. "I'm getting kind of sick of it, to tell you the truth. We were having a nice time, and now you're ruining it." She could hear his footsteps crunching on the sand, closer behind her. The footsteps stopped. Hannah whirled around.

Colin stood in front of her, his eyes fixed on the boat. His face was ashen. The dark circles stood out under his eyes as if crayoned there. Then his hands flew up and gripped the sides of his head with both hands, squeezing tightly as if to squash his thoughts deep into his brain.

Hannah swallowed, staring at him.

"Stop," Colin said in a strangled tone. "Stop it."

Hannah lurched backward a little and her calves bumped the boat, which floated another foot or so into the marshy water.

"Stop, stop!" Colin shouted. "Stop, why are you doing this to me?" He pulled his hair with both hands so that the golden blond strands stuck out as if he'd been electrocuted.

Anger combined with fear suddenly welled up in Hannah's throat. "Why are you doing this *to me*?" she screamed back. "I haven't done anything! *You're* the one with something wrong, Colin!"

Colin groaned, still squeezing his head, then leaned over with one hand on a pine tree and vomited in the sand. Hannah gasped. Then Colin looked up. His eyes were blazing like coals. "This is all your fault," he growled. "Your fault, you stupid bitch." He took a step toward her. Hannah whirled around and ran past him, leaving the boat floating partially in the water. *Get the keys, get in the truck, and get out of here. And go home.* She pounded up the stairs to the house and grabbed the car keys from the kitchen table. She ran through the living room and out the front door, not stopping to look behind her.

Her feet crunched on the gravel of the yard. She wrenched open the truck door, her heart pounding out of her chest. Colin appeared around the side of the house, his knees crusted with sand, his face white and hollow. The blank look filled his eyes. Her hands shaking, Hannah twisted the key in the ignition and waited for the confident roar of the engine. But nothing came. She twisted the key again. Just a clicking noise. Again. Still nothing. The engine was dead. From the corner of the house, Colin stood silently watching.

Hannah sat in the car for a long moment, hands on the steering wheel, staring straight ahead through the windshield. She was trapped. She licked her lips, slowly opened the door and climbed down.

She stood facing Colin. His form was visible as only a blur topped with the shadowy circle of his face. "The truck's not fixed," she finally said.

He didn't reply. He didn't move. His hands hung at his side like hams, like pieces of useless meat.

"You said you'd fixed it."

No reply. He slid his hand into his shorts pocket and pulled out a small gray box, smeared with grease. Hannah recognized it as the thing he'd been yanking at under the car hood and for a moment, she stared at it uncomprehending. Then, with a queer rushing noise in her ears, she looked up into Colin's blank face. "You deliberately sabotaged the car," she whispered through dry lips. She was numb, oddly distant, as if she were observing herself from several feet away.

Colin's face didn't change. He stared at her. *Through her*, she thought. Her mouth filled with sour saliva. All of a sudden, she turned and ran back up the steps into the house, down the shadowy hallway and into the bedroom. Fingers trembling, she slammed the door, twisting the old-fashioned key lock, then leaned back against the door, panting. The numbness was gone. Now her mind whirled feverishly. He wasn't well, she'd been wrong. He was sick, oh my God, he was so sick. He'd gone crazy, she realized. With that realization, her breath left her as if she'd been punched. Her boyfriend had gone crazy. Her legs were shaking and she grasped at the edge of the bedside table for support.

She waited for the sound of heavy footsteps, pressing her head close to the door. But the hallway was silent. Slowly, Hannah sank down on the bed. Her knees ached with adrenaline. She had to get out of here, somehow. *There was no truck. Swim across the lake? Way too far. And who even knew what was on the other side?*

The room was very quiet. Hannah strained to listen for sounds of Colin in the house, but she heard nothing. Moonlight flooded the window, painting the tumbled white sheets with its glow and reflecting off the uncovered lens of Colin's camera on the bedside table.

On a sudden hunch, Hannah picked it up and turned it on. She stared at the screen on the back. A picture of the rowboat on the beach, taken from several feet away, at night. The flash lit up the old wood, the faded red and white paint standing out against the ink-black of the lake water. Rain dotted the camera lens. She forwarded to the next picture. The rowboat again—this time from closer up. And the next. And the next. Hannah pressed the button faster and faster, a sick feeling twisting her stomach. Her hands were cold, clammy. Every picture. Dozens. All at night. All of the rowboat.

Hannah set the camera down next to her on the bed, carefully, as if it might turn into a live snake. *Last night, when he was gone. This is what he was doing. He was out there, photographing the boat, over and over.* Hannah's chest was tight. It was worse than she'd thought. She didn't want to know more. She wanted to crawl under the bed and hide until this was all over. But she couldn't—she couldn't. *Be strong,* she ordered herself. She gritted her teeth and, summoning her courage, crept to the window and peered out. Twisting her head and pressing her forehead to the glass, she could just make out a sliver of the beach. Colin was out there, sitting on the ground next to the rowboat. He was rocking back and forth, holding his head in his hands. Back and forth. Back and forth. He didn't stop.

Silently, Hannah withdrew from the window and pressed her back up against the wall, trying to think. Her eyes fell on her cell phone, sitting on the bedside table. That was it. Call for help. She'd call the police or Laurie or someone—anyone to help her and help Colin. A worm of incredulity pushed itself into her mind that this was Colin—*Colin*—and she was about to call the police on him. But she shoved that thought away.

With her heart finally beginning to slow, Hannah grabbed the phone and thumbed the red on button. She waited for the colorful graphics to roll across the screen. But the screen remained stubbornly dark. She pushed the button again. Nothing. The phone felt oddly light in her hand. She flipped it over and gasped.

The back of the phone gaped like an open mouth. The battery cover was missing, broken off roughly, leaving hard, jagged pieces of plastic. And the battery was gone.

Hannah's fingers began to tremble. Colin was trying to keep her here. Trap her. Somewhere in his sick mind, he was coolly, methodically scheming to keep her right here, where he wanted her. She carefully set the phone down beside her on the bed. It would be no use to search for the battery. He could have hidden it anywhere.

Hannah reached down beside the bed for her bag, which she usually kept there. But her fingers encountered only bare floorboards and dust. With a sinking heart, she realized her purse was sitting out on the living room couch—right next to the open back door. Colin would surely hear her if she tried to retrieve it. She'd have to leave without it.

She took another quick glance out the window. Colin was still on the beach, still rocking. But when she left the room, she'd lose sight of him. He could stand quietly in the shadows and reach out and grab her as she went by. Hannah shoved that thought firmly from her mind and grasped the cold metal doorknob. She twisted it and pushed the door open. The door creaked. She froze with her heart leaping into her mouth.

But nothing. The hallway stretched before her, endlessly long and dark. The entrance to the living room was just a shadowy gray square at the end. Flattening herself close to the wall, her breath coming quickly, Hannah stepped out of the room. She crept down the hall. Now she was past the bathroom. Now the child's room. The door was open a crack, but the inside was like a black cave. The living room entrance loomed ahead of her. Her breath came quicker. The palms of her hands were wet and slippery with sweat.

She stopped at the doorway and peered into the living room. The big room was empty. The gloom pressed at the windows. The furniture sat hunched along the walls.

A faint groaning noise came from the corner and for an instant, her breath choked in her lungs. Then she saw the back door, flapping like a toothless mouth, back and forth in the lonely breeze, groaning each time.

The front door stood ajar on the other side of the room, the screen door still closed. Hannah tiptoed over to it. She hunched her shoulders. Her back felt terribly exposed. Any moment, Colin's hand could fall on her shoulders. She reached out and laid her hand on the rough wood of the screen door. It would squeak. She knew it would squeak.

She shoved hard, and, without waiting, flew across the porch, down the steps, and across the lawn with her hair streaming behind her—expecting his hands to grab her, yank her back, and throw her to the ground.

The tall, wet grass slapped at her bare legs. The woods loomed as an impenetrable darkness in front of her. She plunged into the safety of the trees, colliding with the trunks, grasping at the rough bark, and only then did she turn around.

Pine House was faintly lit by the moon. The screen door gaped askew, and for an awful moment, Hannah thought that Colin had ripped it off. Then she realized *she* must have torn it partially from its hinges when she shoved it open. The yard was deserted.

Hannah took a deep, trembling breath, and stepped deeper into the woods. The fleeting thought that Colin had anticipated her and was hiding somewhere among the trees flitted through her mind. Fear threatened to overwhelm her again. *Focus. Stay calm. Stay strong. You need to get out of here, Han.* She had no light. Instinctively, she looked up, searching for the comforting glow of the moon, but black clouds had moved in, blotting it out.

Hannah never imagined such darkness. She could barely see her hand on the end of her arm when she held it out. She took a few steps blindly, until something caught her foot and she tripped, falling heavily against a nearby tree trunk. The rough bark scratched her cheek and something hard dug painfully into her upper thigh. She rubbed the sore spot and her fingers encountered a hard bulge in her jeans pocket.

With a lift of her heart, Hannah pulled out her keys. She'd forgotten she'd stuffed them in there after finding the bikes yesterday. She twisted the tiny aluminum flashlight—the same one Colin had used to see into the shed—until a fitful beam speared the darkness in front of her.

Hannah played the light on the trees. Brief glimpses showed up—tree trunk, branch, tree trunk, grass. She stepped forward, deeper into the darkness, resisting the urge to run back toward the house, cower in the cab of the truck until morning. But Colin could have retrieved the keys from the ignition where she'd left them. Even if she locked herself in, he could get her out in a second. She forced herself another few feet. She needed to get to the main road, get a ride, and get to a phone. But he could find her on the path from the cabin. She'd have to stay in the woods.

She kept stumbling forward. She didn't have much time before Colin realized she was gone and came looking for her. Or until her flashlight battery died out and she was left in utter darkness. She wouldn't be able to see Colin until he had her.

A twig snapped sharply to her right. Hannah jumped, biting back a scream. Without thinking, she turned and fled, fear momentarily overcoming her, turning her insensible as she crashed blindly past the hulking trees, branches tearing at her T-shirt, scratching her arms and face, every touch like Colin's hand grabbing her.

Her breath sobbed in and out of her open mouth. She heard someone whispering as she ran and only after she slowed did she realize it was herself moaning "Oh, please, oh please, oh please" over and over.

Gradually, fatigue overtook her, dispelling some of the unthinking terror, and she slowed from a blundering run to a trot, and then to a walk, leaning over, grasping her side where a stitch had sunk its teeth deeply. The darkness seemed a little fainter to her right. She realized she was walking parallel to the path that led from the house to the road.

Hannah walked on for what seemed like a long time, the endless undergrowth ripping at her ankles. She tried to listen for any footsteps on the road to her right, but she grew too tired to listen very carefully. How long had she been going? An hour? The adrenaline that had buoyed her earlier was gone.

But in spite of her exhaustion, her mind still churned. Colin . . . maybe at his core, he wasn't who she thought he was. She shuddered at the idea that she'd been dating a stranger for the last year. But no, that couldn't be it. He was sick. He wasn't in his right mind. Maybe he was somehow driven to despair by her inability to admit she loved him? Maybe if she'd said it earlier, he would've been soothed somehow. And Pine House itself. *She'd* wanted to come up here, she thought, guilt flooding her. He'd resisted from the start. *Face it, Hannah. You basically dragged him up. You pushed him over the edge.*

But I didn't even know he had an edge, Hannah argued with herself. Once they'd arrived, he seemed fine. Until the night of the storm, when he'd found those papers. Hannah thought again of the soggy clips of newsprint in Colin's hands, the glimpse she'd caught of a dark-eyed, shaggy-browed boy.

Suddenly up ahead the darkness grew fainter. A glimmer of something yellow shone through the trees, along with another glimmer above it, this one very bright. Hannah walked more swiftly, her heart beating fast with anticipation. The road. She'd reached the main road, with a streetlight shining on the reflective dotted yellow line in the center. Thank God, oh thank God. She felt like crying as she stepped out of the woods and onto the unmowed grass that lined the berm. In front of her stretched the flat gray asphalt, empty.

Hannah hopped awkwardly over the drainage ditch, just managing to avoid cutting her leg on the sharp edge of the ridged pipe that stuck out of the grass. The heat from the day radiated from the asphalt up through the soles of her sneakers. She walked to the center of the road and looked up and down. No cars and only a faint streetlight every fifty yards or so to break the darkness. Woods on one side, and empty fields on another.

Some of Hannah's euphoria floated away. But at least she was out of the woods and away from the house, and that was all that mattered. She could see better out here too. She started walking toward town, matching her strides to the edge of the worn asphalt, which crumbled away into the dry grass lining the road.

The wind blew thinly, whistling in the trees. Moisture rose from the ground, coating her skin. Hannah shivered. She wished for a jacket, a cell phone, a cup of coffee, her mother—anything but this desolate road, the empty pastures, and the endless woods on the other side. She shuddered as she looked across at the mass of dark trees. No way was she going back in there.

She strained her eyes for the lights of town ahead. But there was nothing. She knew it was no use looking. Town was miles away. It would take her hours. No farmhouse yet either. But she was bound to see one with lights on soon. Or a car would come along. She'd take either at this point.

Just then she heard the most wonderful sound in the world—the soft roar of an engine and the rumble of tires. Her heart jumped in her chest. Turning around, she saw headlights appear as pinpricks down the road, growing rapidly.

Panicking suddenly that the car would go by without stopping, Hannah almost leaped into the middle of the road, waving her arms. "Stop, stop!" she yelled. "I need help!"

The headlights loomed in front of her larger and larger, until she actually thought the car was not going to stop. Hannah lifted her hand up and squinted against the blinding white lights, which blotted out everything around her. The car screeched to a halt only a few feet from her legs, and she heaved a huge sigh of relief. Someone—anyone—was here, and she was going to get help.

Hannah ran around to the side of what she now realized was a pickup truck—not a car—pulled the door open, and slid into the front seat in one motion, slamming the door behind her. "Thanks," she breathed. "I really need—" She looked over at the driver and froze, her words shriveling in her mouth. Colin gazed back steadily at her from his seat behind the wheel.

CHAPTER 19

Colin's eyes were empty, like dark pits. His face was slack, and his hands were tight on the wheel. Hannah could feel the blood draining from her face. Her body was icy cold. All her muscles felt loose and useless.

Colin threw the truck into reverse. "I knew I'd find you out here," he said, backing rapidly.

Hannah started. Colin's voice was pitched an entire octave deeper than usual. He sounded like a completely different person. Fear clutched at her throat. She shrank back against the door, feeling behind her for the handle. Could she make it if she jumped?

As if reading her thoughts, Colin casually hit a small button next to his steering wheel. He didn't look at her, but Hannah knew he'd just activated the child locks. She was trapped.

Colin put the truck in drive and accelerated back down the road. He drove with both hands on the wheel, staring straight out at the twin beams of the headlights cutting through the night.

Reason with him, Hannah told herself. *See if you can break through this shell. It's your only choice at this point.* She had a strong feeling he was taking her back to the lake house, but she didn't want to think about that. She took a deep breath. "So, where are we going?" she asked. She tried to make her voice sound easy and confident. She almost didn't expect him to answer.

"Back to Pine House," he said without looking around.

Hannah started again at his deep, gravelly monotone. They were driving very fast. The trees flashed by outside. She knew they only had a few minutes before the turnoff into the woods. She forced herself to lean forward. "Colin, hey, look at me. It's me, Hannah. Colin, please." She could hear the tears in her voice. "Colin, you're scaring me so bad. Please stop. Whatever this is, please stop."

Colin turned to face her, and the truck was still speeding through the night. She recoiled at the cold rage on his face. "You want *me* to stop? *Me?* After everything you've done to me this summer?" he spat. "Just shut the hell up, Tamar."

"Tamar?" Hannah whispered. "Oh my God, Colin, please, who's Tamar? Who's Tamar?" Her voice rose behind the tears. He was hallucinating and in his own world, and Hannah felt consumed by a tide of helplessness. The strength she'd managed to summon in the woods threatened to crumble. She couldn't talk to him because he wasn't hearing her, and she couldn't reason with him. She didn't even know who this girl was—Tamar. An ex she'd never heard about? Just then she caught a glimpse of one

177

of the streetlight poles, dangerously near, as the truck drifted to the right. "Colin!" she screamed.

He looked forward and swerved away an instant before they would have slammed into the pole. Hannah sagged against the seat. Colin swung the wheel hard to the left and the truck bumped off the pavement and onto the rutted path to Pine House.

In what seemed like seconds, they were pulling up to the house. Hannah poised herself as Colin turned off the engine. When he opened her door, she was going to run for it. Straight into the woods with no light, and hide flat in the underbrush until morning. She tensed her muscles as Colin opened his door and deliberately walked around to her side. His figure loomed outside her window. He turned the key in the lock and opened her door. He was blocking the way, but Hannah launched herself off the seat, trying to hit him hard enough so that he'd fall to the ground.

But before she'd barely moved, Colin's hand shot out and clamped down on her arm. He forced her from the truck. Hannah could hear his breath coming fast. She stumbled over the gravel, the long grass ensnaring her ankles, struggling to keep fear from overwhelming her mind. This wasn't him. Colin was gone. This wasn't her sweet, gentle boyfriend. This was a stranger with hard, rough hands.

Colin shoved her around the side of the house, almost lifting her off her feet, down through the weedy side yard, and around to the beach.

"Get in the boat," he said, still in that same gravelly voice. "You want to, don't you? Now's your chance."

"The b-boat?" Hannah stammered. "Colin, no, I'm not getting into that—"

He shoved her arm painfully up her back, and she stumbled forward with a cry, her shins colliding with the side of the boat. The black water lapped at her knees. Colin didn't seem to notice.

"Get in." His voice was cold and dead.

The boat rocked in the water as Hannah climbed awkwardly aboard. Colin climbed in after her and, grasping both oars, leaned back. The boat floated away from the shore.

Hannah huddled in the damp bottom with the spray from the oars catching her face. She had to escape—she had to. She pushed away the thought of what Colin—or what used to be Colin—intended to do out here in the water and tried to calculate her chances of making it to shore if she jumped. Colin pulled steadily at the oars. All around them, the water spread like ink. The clouds had lifted and now a half-moon glittered on the surface of the water. The only sounds were the soft *plash* of the oars and the little laps of the water against the boat as Colin rowed smoothly. Hannah didn't dare try to reason with him. Her arm still stung from where he'd grabbed it by the truck—she didn't want to provoke him more.

They'd almost reached the center of the lake. *Now—do it now!* She had to jump before they got any farther from shore. Hannah poised her muscles. She gripped the splintery sides of the boat tightly and stared down at the undulating surface of the water.

Suddenly a large, hard pair of hands grabbed her and flipped her over the side of the boat. Water flooded over her. She scrabbled at the outside of the boat and dug her fingers into the soft splintery wood, ripping off one of her nails. A searing pain shot up her arm. Colin—Colin had dumped her out, her mind screamed. He was going to kill her, oh Jesus, he was trying to drown her.

She floundered in the water, gulping its fishy taste. Colin loomed over her, leaning dangerously on the side of the boat. She saw his hands come up, then down. "No," she managed to gasp before the water closed over the top of her head, shutting out the ragged sound of her own breath and leaving her suspended in a soundless darkness. The pressure on her head was relentless as Colin held her under. She fought wildly, like a fish on a line, thrashing harder than she ever thought she could, her muscles fueled by adrenaline, her lungs screaming and aching. She twisted wildly. For one instant his hands slipped off her wet head. She broke the surface long enough to pull a single breath.

Above her, Colin's face was twisted with fury, unrecognizable. Standing in the boat, he raised an oar over his head as if to smash her back into the water with it. But when the oar came down, Hannah ducked to the right fast, grabbing his arm and pulling at the same time.

Yanked off balance by her grip, Colin stumbled forward, rocking the boat. His shins collided with the edge, and he somersaulted into the water, sending the empty rowboat seesawing wildly. He disappeared under the water, resurfacing an instant later. At the same time Hannah heard a loud hollow *crack*, and

Colin began sinking again. Hannah dimly realized he had hit his head on the underside of the boat as he surfaced and knocked himself unconscious.

Colin's white face was receding rapidly beneath the black surface of the water. With the boat's rocking threatening to throw off her tenuous grip, Hannah gasped out, "No!" She reached out and grabbed Colin, hauling him up. His eyes were closed—he was still unconscious. His head, wet hair plastered like weeds to his forehead, lolled on his shoulder. A giant blue-black welt was rising on one temple. She tried to hold him more tightly under the arm, while treading water and gripping the boat with her other arm. She couldn't hold on much longer. Already, her arm and shoulder were on fire. Her muscles shook uncontrollably. She was going to have to let him go—or go under herself.

Her breath sobbed in and out of her throat. Colin, this was Colin. He was sick, and he needed help. If she could just get him to shore before he woke up. Before he tried to hurt her again. She could leave him on the beach and take the truck for help. But she could feel her fingers slipping from the edge of the boat. She gasped and hung on tighter. Her finger throbbed like a cancer. Colin's eyes were delicately closed, and his perfect lips and nose were cut as if from marble. Hannah sobbed. "Colin . . . ," she whispered. "Please, Colin, please. . . ." What she was pleading for, she didn't know, but at that moment, as she leaned forward, his eyelids flew up like window shades, looking directly into hers.

Startled, Hannah screamed and thrashed away, instinctively releasing her grasp. Colin coughed and choked. Hannah pedaled her arms, kicking wildly. If Colin was awake, then he was dangerous. As fast as she could, she struck out for shore. It was like swimming through mud. Her sweatshirt and shorts dragged. Her sneakers seemed to weigh thirty pounds each. She tried to kick them off as she swam but they were cemented to her feet. She pulled hard with her arms, coughing each time the rank lake water splashed her face. She could hear Colin swimming behind her. *He was coming for her. Dear God, he was coming for her. Faster. Faster. Just a little bit more. Come on, there's the shore now. Just a few more strokes.*

Her feet found the muddy bottom, and she staggered, trying to swim and run through the last remaining feet of water. Colin was close behind. She could hear his heaving breath. *The sand.* She was on dry ground. *Run, run, run.* She took two giant steps before her feet tangled. She fell to the sand and rolled on her back just as Colin's figure rose over her. She squeezed her eyes shut.

Then his hands closed over hers, tightening on her fingers. Hannah's body tensed, waiting for whatever happened next. She felt a firm tug on her hands and her eyes flew open. With a heave, Colin hoisted her to her feet. The moon shone on his face, and he stared into her eyes. His own eyes were alive again and clear. She could see all the way to the bottom.

The fear that had consumed her for the last hours drained away, and she was filled only with exhaustion and, at the back of her mind, the tiniest glint of hope. She searched Colin's face for any sign of the cloud that had covered him for the day. She found none.

Hesitantly she squeezed his fingers. She felt him squeeze back. His eyes burned into hers, and then he pulled her to his chest, hugged her against him, and burst into tears.

CHAPTER 20

The room was cool and white. In the hallway, the nurses' rubber-soled shoes squeaked against the linoleum. Outside the large window, Hannah could see a neat, green lawn, framed by distant trees. A gardener was slowly pushing a hand mower from one end of the lawn to the other, leaving behind wide green stripes, as if he were vacuuming a rug. Hannah could just hear the distant whine of the motor.

Colin lay in bed, a rough white sheet pulled up to his chest. His eyes were still closed. The lump and bruise on his forehead were now covered by a large white bandage. His hair was dry and swept back from his forehead, and he wore a clean white T-shirt.

Hannah leaned back in her chair. She felt much better since shedding her wet, smelly clothes. One of the nurses at the tiny county hospital had lent her a spare sweat suit she'd had in her locker. It was a little big, but smelled pleasantly of clean laundry, and the soft gray fabric brushed her arms and shoulders like rabbit fur. She rolled her neck around, feeling each kink in her sore muscles.

Soft early-morning sun filtered through the window, turning the room into a light box, but the events of the night before loomed in Hannah's mind—black and cold and windy. Colin, barely able to walk, staggering and sobbing, clutching at her. She'd managed to get him to the truck and into the seat before he passed out. She'd bumped down the dirt road as fast as she dared, shivering in her wet, muddy clothes while Colin sat slumped next to her with his eyes closed and his head lolling on his shoulders.

Out on the main road, she'd had a moment of panic, not knowing whether to drive to Oxtown and hope to find a doctor there or to turn the other direction and drive the forty miles to the interstate. In the end she took a chance and sped through the lonely night toward town, almost fainting herself when she spotted the small blue sign with the *H*. At the tiny cinderblock hospital, floating with exhaustion herself, she'd managed to choke out a version of Colin's symptoms before he was wheeled away. She prayed they wouldn't call the police. Even if he was still dangerous, he needed medical help—not jail.

Her thoughts were interrupted as Colin turned his head back and forth restlessly in the hospital bed, then he groaned a little and opened his eyes. Hannah inhaled, tensing. Colin looked around blearily.

"Hi," Hannah said softly. "How do you feel?"

"Okay," Colin said raspily. He licked his dry lips, and Hannah offered him a glass of water with a bendable straw. He took it and swallowed thirstily. He was so white. The dark circles stood out like charcoal under his hunted eyes. He leaned over in the bed. "Han, what's wrong with me?" he whispered. "Am I crazy?" He put his palm to his forehead as if feeling for a fever. "I remember the lake and the water was so cold, and you were there . . ."

Hannah laid a tentative hand on his arm, covered by the sheet. "It's okay. Shhh. You should rest."

Colin shook his head and pushed himself up in bed. "No, I want to talk." His voice was stronger now.

"Do you remember anything more?" Hannah swallowed. She wasn't sure if she wanted to hear the answer.

Colin nodded, his eyes searching her face. "I wanted to hurt you," he said slowly. "More than that . . . I wanted to kill you." He sat up, and his face was agonized. "Oh my God, Han, what's wrong with me? *Am* I crazy?"

Hannah hesitated. "I . . . don't know." She made herself look him full in the face. "You look like yourself right now. But a lot of awful stuff happened. Maybe the doctor can explain it." She could see the tears brimming on his eyelids. She leaned forward and put her hand on top of his. "Do you *feel* like yourself?"

Colin looked at her straight on. "Yeah, I do. That's what's weird. I would never, ever want to hurt you." His eyes were still his own, and Hannah felt a powerful rush of gratitude. *Thank you. Thank you for letting him be okay right now.* She didn't know if he was going to stay himself or relapse again, but for right at this moment, at least, her own Colin was here. She reached out and clasped Colin's hand with both her own. Hannah leaned down on the bed, bowing her face to hide the tears that welled suddenly to her eyes.

But before she could say anything more, the door behind them opened and a ponytailed young doctor walked in, holding a chart and a legal pad. "Awake, I see?" She smiled, taking a small flashlight out of her pocket. "I'm Dr. Morris, the psychiatrist on call. How's the head feel?" She shone the light briefly in each of Colin's eyes and then flipped through the chart. "The attending says you have no skull fracture and no concussion, Mr. Byrd. Physically, you're in good shape."

She stuck the chart on the end of the bed and came around next to Colin, settling herself in a chair identical to Hannah's. "It's the psychological symptoms I want to talk to you about, but perhaps you'd rather wait until your parents arrive. We've called them, by the way. They should be here shortly."

A shudder ran over Colin at the mention of his parents. "If you don't mind, I'd rather talk now. And I want my girlfriend to stay too." He squeezed Hannah's hand.

Dr. Morris shrugged and flipped to a page of dense notes on her legal pad. "Well, you're eighteen, so the decision is yours." She squinted down at the notes. "Now, from the history your girlfriend gave us last night, I have a rough idea of what happened to you and why."

"What's wrong with me? Am I—," Colin broke in. He looked up at Dr. Morris and faltered a little, then forced the word out. "Crazy?"

Hannah looked anxiously at Dr. Morris, trying to divine her

answer, but the doctor only smiled a little and shook her head. "Colin, it's clear you've gone through a terrible experience—and you too, Hannah. But it's also clear to me that you're not crazy." She paused a moment to let her words sink in.

Relief passed over Colin's face. Hannah exhaled a breath she didn't realize she'd been holding.

Dr. Morris went on. "I believe what you experienced was a period of psychosis, a psychotic break, if you will. An episode like this can be brought on by many things but usually it is some sort of sudden trauma or the reminder of a past traumatic event. It can also be triggered by the sudden resurfacing of repressed memories." She looked down at her notes. "Now Hannah said that you began behaving oddly after a storm, out at your vacation home, is that right?"

Colin nodded.

"And do you remember anything that happened that night that was out of the ordinary?"

"Other than a tree crashing through a window?" Colin laughed a little and glanced at Hannah. His face grew serious. "Yeah, I found something. A newspaper clipping."

Hannah flashed back to Colin crouched on the floor of the child's bedroom, the wet papers in his hand.

Dr. Morris poised her pen over the pad. "And what about that was upsetting?"

"Um . . . I can't remember." Colin didn't meet her eyes.

The doctor gave Colin a sharp look but apparently decided not to pursue the question. "Well, perhaps you'll recall later. To continue, psychotic breaks can also be triggered by contact with the place of trauma—for instance, if you were kidnapped and held in a certain place, returning to that place years later could cause this sort of episode."

Hannah interrupted. "But what about the way Colin was acting? He was so strange—calling me 'Buggy,' making us sleep in the other room—even talking different. Why would just remembering something bad make him act like this?"

Dr. Morris settled herself more deeply into her chair. "Well, psychotic episodes can also include delusions, which I believe Colin was experiencing. People who have delusions can spend extended amounts of time believing they are another person. Then they take on the personality of this person. Delusions are a coping mechanism when the person cannot handle the memories of the extreme trauma they've experienced. Delusional people may also hear voices in their heads, directing their actions."

Colin inhaled a little, as if in recognition, but Dr. Morris, focusing on her notes, did not notice.

"But wait," Hannah said. "If the night of the storm was what caused the um, psychotic-whatever-it-was, then why did Colin get so weird earlier? He had a freak-out during a hike to this old church . . ."

"Well, I can't be completely sure," Dr. Morris said. "But my best guess is that if this vacation house—"

"Pine House," Colin supplied.

"Yes, Pine House—was the place of a past trauma for Colin, any contact with this place caused tiny cracks in the memory façade you, Colin, maintained within yourself. These cracks would widen the longer you stayed at the house. Does that make sense to you?"

Colin nodded. "Yeah, it does. And then the night of the storm—"

"Everything just blew wide-open," Hannah interrupted.

Everyone was quiet in the room for a moment—so quiet that Hannah could hear the wheeze of the automatic doors out in the hallway.

Dr. Morris clicked her pen closed and stood up, tucking her legal pad under her arm. "The good news, Colin, is that this kind of psychotic episode is usually isolated and without afteref-fects. I expect you will recover fully, though I do recommend you begin some sort of counseling when you return home. You'll need help to process this experience." She patted Colin's shoulder. "I'll check back later. Let me know if you'd like me to speak with your family when they arrive."

After the door whooshed closed behind her, Colin gripped Hannah's hand more tightly, like he was holding a lifeline. "Han, I didn't want to say too much in front of the doctor, but I'm com-pletely freaked out. It's so strange what's happening in my mind right now."

"What? Colin, what is it?"

Colin shifted restlessly in the bed. "I'm remembering things."

"Like what about happened in the lake last night?" Hannah asked.

Colin nodded uncertainly. "That part is kind of hazy still.

But. . . . I'm remembering things from my past. Things I never remembered before—about Jack." He squeezed her hand tighter.

"Your brother?" Hannah blinked. "Why?"

Colin stared at the ceiling. "You know Jack was eight years older than me."

Hannah nodded.

"And that he disappeared hiking in the mountains seven years ago—at least that's what my parents always told me."

"Wait," Hannah broke in. "What do you mean, that's what they always *told* you?"

Colin seemed to force himself to look her in the eyes. "The fact is, we never talk about it at home at all—I mean like never. My parents hated it if I ever brought it up. I learned pretty fast that Jack was one of those subjects you just don't discuss."

Hannah nodded. In the back of her mind, she wondered where this was going.

Colin went on. "Han, this house—Pine House—that was another thing we never discussed in my family. I mean, I knew we used to come up here when I was little, but I didn't remember it. My parents always said what I told you—that it was just a decaying old wreck of a place and they'd rather not come up here. Ever."

"Okay . . ." Hannah felt a vague sense of foreboding. "But why didn't they just sell it?"

He shrugged. "I don't know. Maybe they tried and couldn't. It's not exactly prime real estate."

Hannah nodded. "Go on."

Colin pushed himself up on the pillows and reached out for Hannah again. He held both her hands in both of his and stroked her palms with his thumbs, looking down. Hannah waited. Outside the window, the mowing noise went on and on.

After a minute, he spoke again. "I felt weird when you showed me the picture and the old map up in the attic and in the car. I felt like there was something wrong, something nibbling at the corner of my mind. I knew it was stupid though, so I tried to ignore it."

Something clicked in Hannah's mind. "You left the photo of Pine House by the side of the road on purpose, didn't you?"

Colin nodded. "Yeah. I just felt like I didn't want them in the car with me—they were like a box of cockroaches or something. Maybe it was the start of one of those cracks in my memory. But once we got to the house, things were fine. We were having a good time, right?"

Hannah nodded. "Until the night of the storm." She waited, holding her breath a little.

"Right, the storm." Colin traced a little pattern on the bedspread. "I woke up in the middle of the night, and I couldn't go back to sleep. So, I thought I'd go in and clean up some of the mess from the tree branch. But I never got around to it because when I started picking up the papers from the desk in there— the room that used to be mine—I saw this old newspaper clipping. It was a little article from the county paper about the Eat n'Meet café, dated seven years ago. Just an interview, but they had a shot of the dining room with Mike, the owner. And in the background at the counter, there was this dark-haired young guy. Jack. When I saw that article, it was like something broke open in my mind. And that's the last thing I remember really clearly. After that, things get kind of hazy. And this next part is why I didn't want to talk about this in front of the doctor."

Hannah stared at him, her eyes big. "What?"

"The date on the clipping. The month, actually. The article was dated July, but Jack had died in May."

"What?" Hannah frowned. "I don't get it, Colin. How could he be in the newspaper picture if he was dead?"

His hand tightened on hers. "I *thought* Jack was dead. Now I know that's not true. Ever since coming here last night, all of these new memories have floated up in my mind. Just like the doctor said. Repressed memories."

The sheet moved under Hannah's elbow. She looked down and saw Colin's fingers slowly gathering the fabric up until he held it tightly in two fists.

"Jack wasn't dead—at least, not when my parents said he was," he said. "The summer I was eleven, we were at Pine House, and he was there too. I remember this now, as clearly as anything."

He paused and Hannah squeezed his clenched fist. "It's okay."

His clear blue eyes gazed steadily out the window. The gardener was gone now, and the grass was as neat as a putting green. "I wandered around by myself a lot that summer—I was just starting to get into photography, so I took my camera and went for walks, looking for cool things to photograph. One evening I went all the way to that old church, the one we visited, and I stayed late. Then I got a little lost coming back and by the time I found my way back to the house, it was pitch black. I was going around to the back door when I heard voices coming from the lake, carrying across the water. I realized that it was two people in the rowboat, pretty far out."

"Jack?" Hannah interrupted.

Colin nodded. "And his girlfriend, Tamar. She worked at the café in town, and he'd been seeing her all summer. That's probably why he was in that photo in the article. I think she was some kind of runaway—she was just passing through. Anyway, Jack had a temper and she did too. They were always having these wild arguments and then making up. I think my parents were concerned about how they would feed off each other."

"So you heard them in the boat. . . . ," Hannah prompted.

"Yeah. They were arguing again. Jack was shouting and she was shouting back and it sounded like maybe crying too. There was a full moon, so I could just make them out. I saw Jack grab Tamar, like he was going to hit her. I shouted out to stop him, but he either didn't hear me or he was ignoring me. By now Tamar was screaming. So I just kicked my shoes off and went in." Two red spots were burning on Colin's cheekbones. His hands still gripped the sheets.

Hannah leaned forward. "You just swam in? What did you think you were going to do?"

Colin shrugged. "Stop them, I guess. Like an eleven year-old kid was going to stop anything. But I wasn't thinking about that. He was going to hurt her, and I had to stop it. I swam out to the boat, but when I was almost there, I saw Jack force Tamar over the side. He was holding her under—Han?"

Hannah felt sick. She knew Colin could see it on her face. There was a long silence. Then he reached his hand out and touched her cheek. "I know," he almost whispered. "Just like last night."

Hannah nodded mutely.

Colin picked up the pink plastic pitcher by his bedside and poured himself another glass of water. "Want some?"

Hannah shook her head.

Colin downed the water in one gulp. "I don't even remember swimming the rest of the way. The next thing I knew, I was hanging on to the edge of the boat, screaming at Jack to go get help. At the same time, I kept ducking under the water, trying to look for Tamar's body, maybe get her to the surface in time to save her. And Jack . . . he was hanging over the edge of the boat too, screaming back at me that it was all a mistake and she'd fallen over, but the police would never understand. But even in the midst of all of that, I knew he was lying—he'd forced her over, I'd seen it with my own eyes. And I think I was yelling back that this was murder, didn't he understand, and that I was going to get our parents and the police—" Colin suddenly stopped talking.

"Then what?" Hannah realized she was leaning forward, holding the edge of the bed so tightly her knuckles were white.

Colin closed his eyes. "He grabbed me, forced my head under the water. I felt something bump me and opened my eyes . . . Tamar's body was right there, floating next to me. I saw her face. . . ." He paused. "I'd never seen a dead person before."

The room was silent. Out in the hall, a loudspeaker said, *"Paging Dr. Schmidt. Please pick up line one."*

After a time Colin went on. "I played dead. I didn't know what to do. I just went limp and after a second I guess Jack thought I was dead too—or at least unconscious. I felt him release me. I stayed underwater as long as I could, and when I surfaced, I saw him rowing away, toward that wooded part of the shoreline where we came out from the woods the other day."

"Where you had that freak-out I was telling the doctor about."

Colin rubbed the back of his hand across his mouth. "Yeah." He closed his eyes, as if summoning up the memories. "I had to let Tamar's body sink. It was so heavy, and I didn't have much strength left. I made it to the beach by the house the same time Jack made it to shore. He saw me on the beach—he turned and looked right at me. So he knew I wasn't dead. Then he ran into the woods."

Hannah sank back into her chair as if all her bones had been wrung out. "Oh my God, Colin, I can't believe this. I can't believe your own brother tried to kill you." Her voice broke. Colin sat up and awkwardly wrapped his arms around her.

"It's okay," he said into her hair, his voice muffled. "It's okay now, at least."

Hannah sat back, wiping away the tears that had risen to her eyes. She held Colin's hand tightly. "What happened next? Did you go in and tell your parents?" She shivered at the thought of skinny little eleven-year-old Colin, wet and cold and afraid on the beach, all by himself.

Colin's forehead creased. "Yeah, I think I did. Things get a little hazy after that. I went in—my mom was on the sofa, reading, and my dad was in the kitchen. I tried to tell them what happened. I probably wasn't making much sense—wasn't explaining myself well. They just kind of looked at me funny and told me to go to bed and that they'd take care of everything. I was exhausted. I tried to stay awake but I couldn't and, in the middle of the night, they woke me up and rushed me out of the house. We piled into the car and drove home at light speed. They wouldn't say anything about what was going on."

"Why would your parents rush out like that?" Hannah interrupted. "Wouldn't they want to stay and find Jack?"

Colin's brows creased. "No, I think maybe Jack got in touch with them that night and told them what happened. They realized the only way to protect him was to leave. I don't know though. Everything is so mixed up in my mind. It seems like all this was just a dream."

"But it wasn't," Hannah said.

"No." Colin plucked at the sheet again. "I do remember asking over and over where Jack was. But all they said was that I'd been sick, very sick, and I'd been imagining things. Jack had died four months earlier, they said. They'd decided not to go to the house this summer, they told me, because I was in such shock from my brother's death."

A chill ran up the back of Hannah's neck. She shivered. "They were lying, right?"

Colin looked unsure for a minute. "I . . . I don't know. I mean they were my parents, and they were completely adamant that this is what happened. I was just a kid. After awhile . . . I guess I just believed them. It was like it never happened, until the night of the storm." He sat forward, his face intense. "After I saw the clipping, it was like this fuzzy curtain just dropped over my mind. I don't remember anything else from this weekend, except that I was so *angry*. I never knew it was possible to feel that pissed off."

"That was the break Dr. Morris was talking about," Hannah breathed. The pieces were clinking into place one by one in her mind. He hadn't been acting like himself since the storm because he'd been acting like *Jack*. He actually believed that he *was* his brother, Jack, a delusion. And the scene in the rowboat. Colin was reenacting that whole awful night. "Inhabiting Jack's body," Hannah said. "And thinking that I was Tamar." She looked at Colin. "Do you really not remember any of this?"

Colin shook his head. "No. Just a few flashes here and there. I remember working on the truck. I wanted to take out the relay so it wouldn't start, but I don't know why. It was like someone else was in my head, telling me to do it—voices, like the doctor said. The cell phone too. I knew I had to take out the battery and flush it down the toilet, but I didn't know why."

"Jack. Jack was telling you to do it." A shudder ran through Hannah. "You had to keep me there."

"*Jack* wanted to keep you there," Colin reminded her. "It wasn't me."

There was a knock at the door. Hannah sat up fast. A burly orderly poked his head in. "Your parents are here, Colin." There was rustling in the hallway behind him.

. Colin's body tensed. "Han, stay with me," he whispered hoarsely. "I don't know how I can see them. Don't leave."

"I won't. I'm here." Her voice sounded far stronger than she felt. How could Colin even look at his parents, knowing what he knew now? This was all happening so fast. She wished he could have some time to absorb everything the doctor had said, but they were right here. Hannah squared her shoulders and took a deep breath.

The orderly shoved the door open further and stood aside as Mrs. Byrd pushed past him and rushed at the bed. She wore a trench coat thrown over an expensive sweat suit. Colin's father followed closely behind, his face gray.

"Colin, are you all right?" his mother said, bending over his bed and grasping his shoulder. "We were frantic when the hospital called. What happened? What are you doing up here?" She sat down on the edge of the bed. His father clustered in behind. Colin took a firmer grasp on Hannah's hand. She squeezed back, hoping he could feel the strength flowing through her fingers to his.

Colin looked right at his mother. Hannah recoiled a little at the cold conviction in his eyes. "Mom, I have to talk to you. And Dad, too." His voice was steady, but Hannah heard the tremble underneath.

"What is it?" His mother's hand went to her throat.

Colin pushed himself up a little in bed. "Mom, I know."

Mrs. Byrd froze. "About what, darling?" Her eyes glittered.

Colin's face was expressionless. "About Jack. And that summer."

Mrs. Byrd made a strangled little noise in her throat. Then her face smoothed over, reminding Hannah of a curtain dropped over a stage. His father gripped his mother's shoulder. Colin went forward relentlessly. "Some stuff has happened to me the last couple of days that I'd rather not talk about. All I want to say to you is that I know that Jack didn't die in the mountains. I know he tried to drown me in the lake, after he killed Tamar. I know how you tried to cover it up and how you lied to me."

His mother was shaking her head back and forth slowly, over and over. "No, Colin, no, no," she kept saying.

Colin stared fixedly out the window. Hannah tapped his hand. He turned his head toward her. *It's okay,* she mouthed. He nodded and gave her a faint smile.

His mother kept shaking her head. Then she grew still. The room was quiet for a long time. Mr. Byrd sat as if carved from stone and his eyes were shiny, though whether it was from grief or rage, Hannah couldn't tell.

Then Colin's mother sat up straight. She lifted her head and cleared her throat. "Colin, you're in shock." Her voice sounded overly loud in the small room. Hannah inhaled sharply. His mother went on. "Why would you say these horrible things? Why would you accuse us, your own parents, of deceiving you?" Her lips were a thin slash in the white dough of her face. "It's unnatural, saying that we would lie to you for years and years." Her tone changed and became silky, like pudding. "You've had a terrible shock, dear. I can see that. You need rest, and then we'll get you home and get you help. Medicine, perhaps." The soft tone grated on Hannah's nerves more than any of Mrs. Byrd's iciness.

A drop of something fell to the floor. Hannah looked over. A thin stream of blood was trickling from Mrs. Byrd's clenched fist and dripping slowly onto the old linoleum.

CHAPTER 21

The house was dim and quiet when Hannah slipped her key from the lock that evening. Behind her, Colin's parents' car backed down the driveway and chugged off down the street. After he was discharged, Colin had tried to tell his parents that he would drive the truck home with Hannah, but Mrs. Byrd insisted on driving together. Colin's father would return later to retrieve the truck, she said. As they left the hospital Colin informed them that he did not want to discuss any part of the last two days, and so the ride home had been tense and miserable, with Colin sitting like a statue in the backseat beside her and heavy silence filling the car.

"Mom?" Hannah called into the interior. The front table was piled high with mail. A pair of David's sneakers tangled with his backpack lay on the hall rug. They looked very small and the sight of them made Hannah call louder into the house, *"Mom? Anyone there? Dave?"*

Her mother's familiar figure darkened the doorway to the

kitchen, holding a stick of butter in one hand. "Hi, honey! How was the trip?" Her face creased with lines as she smiled and held her arms out.

With a thump, Hannah dropped her backpack from her shoulder and ran into her mother's arms, squeezing her around the back and burying her head into the crook of her mother's neck and shoulder. "Hi," she said, her throat aching as she tried to hold back the tears. A few escaped, trickling down her cheeks and wetting the collar of her mother's work shirt.

"Han?" Her mother pulled back, gazing intently into her daughter's face. "What's wrong? Did you and Laurie have a fight?"

For an instant Hannah couldn't figure out why her mother was asking about Laurie, but she caught herself just in time. She took a deep, trembling breath and swiped at her cheeks. "No . . . nothing like that."

Mom gave her a long, searching glance but turned back to the kitchen without saying anything more. "I was just making grilled cheese for us. You hungry, hon?" She clattered the frying pan back onto the stove.

The kitchen smelled deliciously of melted cheese. David sat at the table, his face three inches from a comic book spread out in front of him, his hair standing up as usual. "Hi," he said without looking up. "Mine's the one with bacon. If you want bacon, you better tell Mom."

Hannah sat down in the chair next to him and knotted her fingers to keep herself from grabbing him into a hug. Instead she settled for nudging his foot under the table. "I'm just going to eat yours, is that okay?"

David's head jerked up. "Mo—," he started to say before he looked at Hannah's face. "Stop teasing."

"Never." This time she gave in and, reaching over, squeezed him into a headlock-hug.

"Moooom!" He flailed his skinny arms.

"Han, stop," her mother said absently. "You want tomato on yours?"

"Mmhmm." Hannah watched her mother's bony fingers steady the tomato on the cutting board and slice with slow, steady strokes. She was using the bread knife, like she always did.

Mom placed a slice of tomato on the toast piled with cheese and turned around; her eyes were concerned. "Han, are you sure you're all right? You don't seem . . . quite yourself tonight."

Hannah closed her eyes, trying to shut out the black water floating in her mind. The trickle of blood flowing onto the worn hospital floor. "No," she said slowly. "It's been a strange couple of days."

Hannah's cell rang just as she was climbing into bed that night. She pulled the quilt up to her chin and glanced at the screen. It was him. Her heart thumped suddenly, even though there was really no reason she should be nervous.

She clicked the phone on. "Hi," she whispered.

"Hey there." His voice was strong and casual.

There was a long pause. Hannah's tongue felt frozen. There

were so many questions she wanted to ask him—*Are you still okay?*
Are you still Colin? What happens now?—but the words crowded
up against her teeth and were imprisoned there.

Instead she said, "Are you packing?"

"How's your mom?" Colin asked at the same time.

They both laughed.

Hannah cleared her throat. "Mom's fine. She didn't suspect
a thing."

"Oh, good. Yeah, I'm all packed. My flight's at three tomorrow."

Another pause. Hannah heard the shuffle of papers on the
other end. "Are you reading something?"

"Yeah, I just got out a bunch of Jack's old papers and stuff
from the attic. I'm trying to learn about him some." He sounded
uncomfortable and formal.

"Oh wow, yeah. Good idea."

"Yeah. It's like a part of my life has opened up that I didn't
even know existed. I'm curious about what's happened to him
since, you know, that summer."

"It's weird to think he might be still out there." Hannah
looped her arms around her knees and the blankets pooled
around her waist.

"Or dead."

"Right, or dead." There was an awkward little pause, and
then Hannah cleared her throat. "Um, this feels weird. This conversation, I mean."

"Yeah. I know."

She waited for something more, but that was all he said. She threw back the covers and went over to the window, leaning her forehead on the cool pane of glass. "Well, listen, I'm meeting Laurie at the Sunporch Café tomorrow at ten, so—"

"Oh, yeah, great. I'll come meet you to say good-bye."

"Great."

"Great."

Another silence.

"Okay, um, so I'm exhausted and—"

"Oh, sorry, yeah. Talk to you tomorrow." He hung up, leaving Hannah holding the dead phone to her ear and her lips still poised to say good night.

Hannah lay back down in her bed and stared up at the ceiling. *Awkwardness with the boyfriend who tried to drown you because he thought he was his own dead brother who turned out not to be dead. Probably not a lot of advice lying around for this particular relationship problem.*

CHAPTER 22

"You look skinny, Han," Laurie said as Hannah dropped into the padded plastic booth across from her the next morning. The diner was noisy. A long line of people waited for brunch with papers under their arms, and steam fogged up the windows. At the front the cash register rang incessantly, and waitresses barreled past the tables with harassed expressions and platters of eggs over easy, biscuits, and bacon.

"I don't know why," Hannah mumbled, grabbing a huge plastic menu and hiding behind it. "I've only been gone since Friday." She peeked out at her friend, who was sitting forward on the edge of her seat, her wet hair tied back in a neat ponytail and her button-down shirt precisely buttoned. She looked ready for battle. Hannah retreated behind the menu again.

"Well," Laurie said, leaning forward, "maybe you look so god-awful because, oh, I don't know—*your boyfriend tried to kill you.*"

"You ladies ready to order?" A waitress with a tight auburn perm stood beside the table with her pad in hand.

"Toast, please. And coffee." Hannah handed the menu over, trying to gauge if she'd heard Laurie's words, but the woman's face was impassive.

Laurie smiled up at the waitress sunnily. "The number two please with bacon and scrambled eggs. And a side of hash browns."

The waitress nodded and scribbled, then hurried away with the menus tucked under her arm.

"What, you're not eating?" Laurie returned to the attack.

Hannah scowled at her. "No, I'm just not hungry."

"Have you talked to Colin since you've been back?"

Hannah bit her bottom lip. "Yeah, he called last night. He's coming by here to say good-bye." She poked her fork through her napkin and looked up to find her friend studying her carefully. "What?"

"Come on, tell me."

Hannah sighed. "How can you always tell when something's wrong? I mean, other than the obvious."

"Years of practice. Spill."

Hannah twiddled the fork between her fingers and stared out the window at a guy feeding a parking meter. "It was such an awkward conversation last night. I felt so weird, like I didn't know what to say to him."

"How about, 'I'd really prefer stabbing to drowning, my dear?'"

Hannah glared. "Not funny."

Laurie rolled her eyes. "Sorry. Look, honestly, how can it *not* be a little awkward between you guys? It wasn't exactly Disneyland up there, from what you told me."

"I know," Hannah muttered. "I just don't want it to end like this."

"Maybe it doesn't have to." Laurie nodded significantly over Hannah's shoulder.

Hannah turned around.

Colin was standing behind her in a pool of sunlight, wearing a backpack. His blond hair was tousled in the front and sticking up at the back, as if he'd just woken up. On one side of his forehead, the bruise was fading to yellow. "Hey there." He smiled, the same charming Colin smile she loved.

"Hi," Hannah said softly.

They looked at each other. Across the room, their waitress was yelling at one of the cooks. A young mom wheeled a giant stroller past their table.

"Well!" Laurie said after a long pause. "I'd better go. You know, work and all." She collected her bag and slid out of the booth. "Bye, lovebirds. Colin, good luck at Pratt."

"Huh?" Hannah tore her eyes away from Colin's long enough to see Laurie hurrying away toward the door. "Wait, what about your breakfast?" she called.

"You still want these?"

Hannah looked around. The waitress was standing at her elbow with the toast and coffee and Laurie's loaded platter.

Hannah lifted her eyebrows at Colin.

"Sure, we want them," he told the waitress. "Now I don't even have to order."

Hannah sat down, and Colin slid in beside her. She watched as he speared a chunk of scrambled egg, and then she took a deep breath. "Colin, I know things were weird on the phone yesterday and—"

"Han—" He tried to interrupt but she held up her hand.

"No, don't deny it, I know you felt it too, and I wanted to just say that we went through a lot this last weekend and—"

"Hannah—"

"—I'm sorry I haven't said anything before now, but—"

"Han!" He raised his voice slightly and a white-haired couple at the next table looked around.

She blinked. "What?"

"I brought you something." He grinned at her and leaned over to unzip his backpack, pulling out a small, flat object about the size of a book, wrapped in brown paper. He placed it on the table in front of them. "I just finished it before I came here."

Hannah stared at it like it was a leprechaun.

Colin pushed it toward her. "Open it."

Cautiously, Hannah slid her finger under the tape and pulled off the paper. She caught her breath. It was a black-and-white photo, on a plain white mat, of a girl's profile in silhouette. Her hair fell over one shoulder like a curtain as she gazed down at something in her hands, her expression intent and absorbed. Behind the girl was a window, making a frame for her face, and through the window, a gorgeous tapestry of lights spread, pin-pricks of white on black, all rolling and tangled as if they'd been tossed by the wind.

"It's me," she breathed, holding the photo gingerly by the edges.

"When we were in the attic last week, remember?" Colin leaned over, smiling. "I snapped it while you were fiddling with your lens."

"Yeah . . . that day seems so long ago." She grinned a little. "It was a long weekend."

Colin nodded. "And there's more hard stuff ahead of us too, since I'm going away. But that's why I made two copies of that photo—one for my dorm wall at Pratt and one for you. This way, you'll know exactly what I'm looking at every night when I go to sleep." His voice cracked a little and his eyes were suspiciously shiny.

Hannah swallowed past the ache that had risen in her own throat. "Colin, I know things will never be the same as they were between us, but I've been sure of something for so long. I didn't want you to leave without knowing that—" She stopped. "I love you."

For a moment he said nothing, and it seemed to her that all the colors of the diner faded to gray. Then he said, "Han, I love you too," and everything burst into glorious focus.

She grabbed him and buried her head in his chest as his arms came around her. He held her, murmuring into her hair, "I can't believe it took you this long."

"I figure that if I still care about you after this weekend, it must be the real thing, right?" she said into his chest.

He laughed. "No one can say we haven't been tested."

Hannah leaned back, gazing up at her boyfriend's face. "Do you really have to leave today?"

He nodded. "I have to. But, Han . . ." His eyes searched hers. "You know that you'll always be with me."

ACKNOWLEDGMENTS

I would like to thank my agent, Michael Bourret, who believed in this book from the start, and my editor, Emilia Rhodes. Her sharp insight showed me what this story could become. And thanks are also due to my dad, whose view of the world has shaped my own, and who appreciates a good scary story as much as I do.

Here's a sneak peek at

CLOSER

a new novel by Emma Carlson Berne

COMING FROM SIMON PULSE

FALL 2012

PROLOGUE

The party had been going on for hours. Megan knew she shouldn't have anything more to drink. Already, the edges of the dark basement room had grown fuzzy, the knots of sophomores and juniors lining the walls and lounging on the floor retreating into a vodka-induced haze. Music pounded from two huge speakers, and shadowy couples grinded together like contortionists, clogging the space in front of the drinks table. Megan looked down at the big plastic cup in her hand and swirled the orange liquid before tilting a little more down her throat. Vodka and orange soda. You'd think it would be nasty but it wasn't too bad.

She stifled a burp against the back of her hand, slowly sliding down the wall until she was sitting on the cream carpet. She could feel the bass vibrating through the floor. She edged herself over a couple inches to the right to avoid a large puddle of salsa seeping into the expensive weave and carefully propped her cup against the wall. At least she wasn't standing by herself anymore. Megan glanced at the clump of juniors sitting to her right—Kelsey, Logan, Maya, all with heavy, silky long hair, the kind that always fell into place, no matter how much you played with it. Megan resisted the urge to smooth her own thin, wavery strands and the cowlick that always rose up into a stubborn curl in the front. She aimed a tentative smile at Logan, who stared back blankly, as if she didn't recognize Megan.

Whatever. They were all Anna's friends anyway.

Megan picked at the carpet, willing the hotness in her face to fade. Anna was in Europe with her parents. "Promise me you'll go to Mike's party," she'd insisted before she left. "He's so sad I'm abandoning him for Europe." She and Megan had been sitting on the wall outside Anna's parents house, eating Funyuns. "Promise! He wants everyone to come—even you." Anna had delicately poked her hand into the bright yellow bag. Even eating greasy onion rings, she'd still managed to look like an Irish princess.

Even you. Megan tried to wrap her mind around the words but the moment had passed. Just like always. "Okay," she'd said. "I will." Of course she would. She always did what Anna asked. Which is why she was here, at Anna's boyfriend's party, alone. Megan gulped the rest of her drink down in one swallow and paused, coughing a little, as the girls sitting beside her seemed to grow larger, then smaller.

Kelsey looked over. "Nice, Megan," she said, grinning and patting Megan on the back.

"Yeah, go crazy!" Maya jumped up, pumping her hips back and forth as she chanted, "Go, Megan, go, Megan, go Megan . . ."

In a far corner of her mind, the sober corner, Megan knew they were making fun of her, but it didn't seem so shameful right then. Just friendly and funny. She giggled and climbed to her feet as the rest of the girls started dancing in a circle, swaying and waving their arms in the air. The heavy, insistent beat of the music pounded in Megan's bones. The space grew more crowded. People pressed in from all sides and Megan gulped for air like a goldfish. Sweat trickled down the side of her neck and into her bra. Surreptitiously, Megan swiped at the front of her shirt just as Mike's bulky figure loomed in the semidarkness like a panther.

"Hey!" Logan greeted Mike with a squeal. The girls widened their circle, making a space for him, but instead Mike slipped behind Kelsey, putting his arms around her waist. They danced like that for a second before Kelsey broke away, laughing. Logan grabbed her by the hands, whispering something in her ear.

The other girls drifted into the mass of people. Not that it mattered. The music was hypnotic now, not jarring. Megan closed her eyes, extending her hands out as she danced, imagining herself as some high-cheekboned hippie chick twirling in front of a stage at Woodstock. In another level of her mind, she congratulated herself for not dancing around like an out-of-sync gerbil.

Someone touched her waist. Megan started to turn, but not before a thick pair of arms slid around her middle. She twisted around and looked up. Mike's face, grinning and sweaty, floated above her. "Having fun?" he shouted over the music. His hands rubbed the small of her back. Megan tried to keep a few inches between them.

"Yeah!" she shouted back. They were practically screaming. "Do you miss Anna?"

"What?" He cupped his ear.

Megan shook her head. It was probably a stupid question to ask at a party anyway. Mike pulled her closer as they danced. His belt buckle dug into the waist of her jeans. *Whoa there.* Megan darted a glance left and right. No one was paying attention to them them. *Don't be so uptight.*

"Hey, you look really pretty," Mike shouted.

Megan glanced down at her white tank top. It had taken her an hour to decide what to wear. "Thanks!" She bit the inside of her cheek to keep from smiling idiotically.

Mike nodded along with the music and ran his hands up and down her back. *Is he coming on to me? Mike? Anna's boyfriend. What is he doing?* His hips ground against hers. *Definitely coming on to me.* He was holding her really close now. She could see the blond stubble on his chin. She'd never danced like this with a guy, not with a big, sexy guy like Mike. It was beyond nice. Actually, it was so beyond nice that Megan could barely keep a coherent thought in her head.

Megan could feel people looking at them now. They were watching her grind with her best friend's boyfriend. Megan knew that with certainty. This was wrong in every sense and she couldn't care less, much less stop herself because Mike's breath was on her face and every fiber of her body, which had completely divorced itself from her mind, was reaching up toward him, as he leaned down toward her.

Then it was happening. It really was. Mike was kissing her. His tongue was in her mouth. Her legs were shaking. She felt like hot oil was running over every inch of her skin.

You are kissing Mike! her mind screamed, but her stubborn, rebellious body refused to listen, just kissed him back with her arms locked around his neck.

Then his grip changed. Mike's hands weren't around her waist anymore, they were around her neck, wrapped around her throat. His thumbs pressed insistently on her windpipe even as he kept kissing her. Megan wrenched her head back and her eyelids flew open like a startled sparrow's as she choked, but he would not let go. *Why is the room was so dark?* Her lungs were tight, screaming for air as he squeezed harder. *Why is his face so blurry?* It didn't even look like Mike, his features looked smaller, softer. It wasn't Mike at all, it was Anna. And Anna's hands were around her neck, squeezing harder and harder as Megan gasped for air, Anna's berry-painted lips stretching in a wide grin because she'd found out, she knew what Megan had done. . . .

CHAPTER 1

The bus bumped over a pothole and Megan woke with a start, jerking her head from the hot pane of glass where it had been resting. She eased the twisted strap of her canvas bag from across her shoulders. It took her a minute to get it off, then she lay her head back against the blue plastic seat. Her heart was hammering like a scared rabbit. What a dream. She sat still, trying to recover, staring at the metal ceiling of the bus, where a red-and white square was marked: IN EMERGENCY, PULL HANDLE, THEN PUSH DOOR OUTWARD. Megan briefly pictured herself standing on the seat, pushing the hatch open. It would be cooler with the wind whipping past.

Mike. God, why was she thinking about *that* debacle? It was over, finished, done with last summer. Megan reached into her khaki tote and pulled out a stainless-steel water bottle. She took a long drink, grimacing at the warm, flat taste. *Don't play dumb,* she told herself. She knew why she was thinking about that night—it was exactly one year ago today. One year ago that she made the biggest mistake of her life. And almost lost her best friend forever. Almost.

To distract herself, Megan focused on the back of the bus driver—straight coffee-colored neck, neat blue polyester collar. The other bus riders seemed practically comatose, beaten into submission by the stench of the clogged lavatory at the back. To Megan's right, a young blond woman cradled a sleeping toddler, the child's head flung back. A girl about Megan's own age sat in front of them, slumped down. Behind Megan, someone was snoring rhythmically, with a sound like a small chainsaw.

The sun beat through the windows, filling the coach with the smell of hot gym shoes, despite the best efforts of the asthmatic air conditioner, which whistled through the vents over their heads. It had been four hours of corn and soybeans under the whitish sky, broken by the occasional truck-stop exit full of belching semis and minivans stuffed with sticky children. But at least Anna was waiting for her at the other end.

Megan dug out her phone and thumbed through Anna's last email, sent yesterday. *"Pick you up in front of the restaurant on the main street. I think it's called The Leaf. The farm looks gorgeous—I can't believe it's been three years since I was last up here. You are going to love it. I'm so excited we get to work together!!!"*

Megan stared out the window. The landscape was starting to get more hilly now, with patches of lush woods flashing past. She had been so excited when Anna asked to work with her on her uncle Thomas's farm this summer. Anna used to go up there every summer, back before her dad left. Then a few months ago, her uncle called and said that her aunt had started using a wheelchair because of her MS and he needed some extra help. Anna had arrived last week to get started.

Megan gazed apprehensively out the window at a giant green tractor trawling slowly up and down a sea of waving corn leaves. No—it wasn't going to be like that. She scrolled through the email again. "—*ten pigs, chickens, a big garden, and horses!*" Anna had written. That didn't sound too bad. More like the Richard Scarry books she used to read when she was little. She scanned the rest of the email. *"And we get a separate place to sleep too, just for the two of us. Oh yeah. There's a surprise too. I won't say too much now, but it's definitely going to make this summer way more fun."*

The bus swayed as the driver guided it around a hairpin turn. They were going into some sort of valley now, with trees crowding right up against the road. Megan caught a glimpse of a rushing creek, more like a little river. She wondered what the surprise was. Anna's surprises could be odd sometimes. Like the time she'd made T-shirts for Megan and her with Mr. O'Gorman's picture on it. He was their eighth-grade history teacher, and they both had crushes on him. Anna thought they should wear the shirts to school. Megan had told her that would be way too embarrassing, which Anna didn't understand at all. She'd said it would be funny. Megan had refused and Anna shredded both shirts with her mother's meat scissors.

The bus reached the bottom of the valley. Black cows stood with their heads buried in knee-high grass, their tails switching.

The other bus riders were waking up, gathering their possessions. The snorer behind her sat up with a grunt and belched. Megan sat up straighter, craning to look through the windshield. She could see nothing but the tops of some buildings partially hidden by a low hill. That must be the town, Ault Flats. Megan felt a wriggle of anticipation in her belly. The driver rolled through a stop sign, made a sharp left, then braked abruptly. He cut the engine and opened the door with a pneumatic hiss. It seemed very quiet without the engine noise. Megan watched the other riders file down the aisle. Megan hitched her messenger bag over her shoulder and wrestled her duffel down from the metal rack overhead. This was it. She was here.

Climbing down the steep black steps, the heat hit her like a furnace blast. It radiated up through the soles of her sandals and pressed against her face. Megan found herself alone on a cracked sidewalk.

Buildings lined either side of the short street—the only road in the town, as far as Megan could tell. There was a worn-out pharmacy, a pawn shop, a barnlike structure with bags of fertilizer stacked out front and a sign reading BAKER'S FEED AND SEED, a repair shop with a disemboweled tractor visible in the open bay, and a liquor store.

Her palms were sweaty and her messenger bag was cutting into her shoulder. Megan changed her grip on her duffel, scanning the buildings for The Leaf. The sun was a pale disk burning through the dull clouds. It was so quiet, Megan's sandals scraped on the gritty sidewalk as she turned around. This place was really remote. She'd kind of been picturing something . . . cuter. And Anna wasn't here. Megan tried to tamp down her annoyance. Maybe the bus had been early. She glanced at her phone. No. Right on time.

A few men with weather-seamed faces sat outside the repair shop, perched on metal barrels. Megan felt their eyes on her legs and she swallowed, trying not to feel self-conscious. She wished she'd worn jeans instead of shorts. Where the hell was the damn Leaf Restaurant? Did Anna have the name wrong or—she spotted a green and white sign across the street with a surge of relief and marched purposefully toward it.

Megan set her bag down between her feet and leaned awkwardly against a windowsill, folding her arms on her chest and trying to look nonchalant. *Don't those gross old guys have anything else to do? Fix some tractors or something?* One with a bushy brown beard, winked at her. Megan gritted her teeth and looked steadily and deliberately at the yellow shop sign next door. J&B PAWN, SINCE 1960.

Just then, she heard the rumble of an engine and saw a rust-red pickup roaring toward her, Anna at the wheel. With immense relief, Megan picked up her bag, a grin already on her face. She stepped to the curb in readiness, waving wildly as the pickup drew near. But Anna didn't stop. The truck roared past. Megan could see Anna turn her head, laughing. She disappeared down the street. Megan's hand wilted by her side and a familiar mixture of frustration and resignation rose in her throat. She stood, her face flaming as the men in front of the repair shop chortled. At the end of the street, the truck screeched in a U-turn and drove back toward her. This time, Anna stopped and Megan ran to the passenger door, wrenching it open in a shower of rust flakes.

"Hey!" Anna said, still laughing. "Got you! Your face when I drove past was hilarious." Her sunglasses covered half her cheeks, like she had huge fly eyes. Her buttery blond hair was twisted on top of her head and she wore a clingy gray T-shirt, and jeans cut off just above her knees.

Megan tucked her tote behind her feet. It was just Anna being Anna. "Those old guys at the garage thought it was hilarious too." Megan kept her voice light.

"You look gorgeous, by the way." Anna reached over and gave Megan a one-armed hug as she drove. "I'm so glad to see you!"

"You too," Megan replied and suddenly, she was. Anna's presence was like a firework—sizzling, bright, colorful. She relaxed back against the seat, which was covered with an old gray blanket, sprinkled liberally with dog hair. She cranked the window down as far as it would go and let the breeze dry her sweat-dampened hair. "This truck is great. Really . . . farm-y."

"Yeah, Uncle Thomas let me borrow it to come get you. And it's a stick shift! Can you believe I'm driving it?"

"No, not really." Megan watched her friend's sneakered feet alternately press the pedals on the floor. "Do I have to drive it?"

"Probably. We use it all the time for hay and feed and stuff." Anna shifted expertly into third gear.

"Oh." A few shreds of straw blew up from the floor of the cab and whirled around her knees. "How's it been so far? It feels like you left way longer than a week ago."

Anna nodded. "I know. *So* much has happened too," her voice bubbled. Megan was about to ask what she meant, but Anna kept talking. "How was home?"

Megan made a face. "Boring. Mom made me take online tours of colleges with her all week."

Anna slowed down behind a trailer full of cows. "Ick. Why didn't you just tell her to stop?"

"Oh, sure. She'd love that. Then you'd be working up here by yourself this summer because I'd be confined to the house." Megan extracted her water bottle again and took a drink. "So, what's it *like*, you know, working on a farm? I'm kind of nervous." For an instant, she wished she could take the words back, before Anna gave her that look like she was the most idiotic person in the world. But her friend just reached out and squeezed her knee.

"It's fun. You'll love it, I promise. Uncle Thomas does all the serious plowing and mowing and stuff. The summer hands mostly do the garden and the chores."

"Chores?" It sounded like a Laura Ingalls Wilder story. They were always doing chores in those books.

"Like feeding the animals and mucking and gathering eggs. And you're getting paid! It's better than Silver Mountain."

They looked at each other and Megan snorted, then they burst out laughing. They'd both applied to work at the Silver Mountain jewelry kiosk in the mall before Thomas had called.

The woman that ran the place looked like she ate high-schoolers for snack.

Megan offered the water to Anna. "Is it weird seeing your aunt in a wheelchair?" she asked sympathetically.

"No." Anna voice was hard. She took a long swig.

Megan raised her eyebrows. "It was just a question." More fences, more cows outside. Clapboard farmhouses with American flags. Children's toys in the driveways. A field of sheep, looking like dingy cotton balls with legs.

Anna sighed, capped the bottle with one hand, and handed it back. "Aunt Linda and I don't really get along, okay? She's never liked me, because I was always Uncle Thomas's favorite. She's jealous." Anna's fingers tightened on the steering wheel.

"Oh." Megan searched her mind for a new subject. Making Anna mad was never a good idea. She glanced at her friend's toned arms. "How is it that you already have a tan?"

Anna's face lightened and she laughed as if she knew how great she looked. "Ten hours in the sun every day? I've mostly been working in the garden this week." The corners of her lips turned up and she lingered over the words, as if drawing up pleasant memories.

"By yourself?"

"No . . . Uncle Thomas has some full-time help. Dave and Sarah. They're, like, twenty-five."

The road was straight now, and the cows had given way to open fields of some kind of low, curly plant. Anna pressed her foot on the accelerator. She gave Megan a significant look.

"Okay, I give in," Megan said. "Come on, what's the surprise? I know you're dying to tell me."

Anna seemed to hold herself in for a moment, then burst out, "Oh my God, Megan, I *met* someone and he's so perfect! I was going to wait and not say anything until later, but I just *have* to tell you. His name is Jordan and he's one of the other summer hands. He started the same time as me, and he's so sweet. We've been hanging out all week and it's getting really serious. I think that he could be, you know, *the one*." She was practically bouncing in her seat, her eyes hot and bright.

Megan could feel sweat break out on her upper lip, despite the breeze from the open window. "Oh, wow!" she said, trying for simple excitement. Anna hadn't gone out with anyone since she and Mike had broken up. No one ever said it was because of what happened at the party, but by the time school started in the fall, Anna and Mike were over. During the initial explosion, Megan had sobbed and apologized. Anna called every single night to tell Megan just how furious she was. Then after one month exactly, Anna never spoke of it again. She would completely shut down when Megan attempted to broach the subject.

Anna watched her, glancing frequently at the road. Megan licked her lips. "That is so great." She felt like she was balancing on a slick stepping stone in the middle of a creek. One misstep and she'd fall in. "I'm really happy for you." If Anna could find someone new, maybe the wound would be healed. The wound Megan had created. A fresh wave of guilt swamped her, somehow undiminished despite twelve months.

Megan reached over and grasped Anna's hand for a second. "I am so happy for you," she repeated, looking right at her friend. *Please, Anna. Believe me. Should I say something more? Like an anniversary apology?*

"Thanks." Anna squeezed Megan's hand and then released it to turn onto a narrower side road. "I'm happy for me too."

The weeks of the summer stretched out like a long, murky river. They would be together every day, sleeping together, eating together. She had to get it out in the open. She had to say something about the anniversary. *Okay. Say it now. "I just wanted to tell you how sorry . . . You know, today is one year . . . I'm so glad we're still friends after . . ."* But the passage of a year weighed on Megan and instead she let out her breath and rested her head against the scratchy blanket. They were quiet for a few miles. The breeze blowing through the window was cooler now, almost refreshing. Trees were everywhere, huge towering oaks and maples with long grass laid over in swathes around their trunks. They passed an old red brick house, like something out of *Pride and Prejudice,* then a mowed pasture with horse jumps. The next house was a massive Tudor concoction surrounded by landscaped grounds. Megan blinked. "I'm sorry, are we in another state? Why does everything look like it's from a Jane Austen novel all of a sudden?"

Anna laughed. "I know, weird, isn't it? It's all farms and cows, and then it turns into this super-fancy area called Ault Hill." They passed a twenty-five miles per-hour sign and Anna slowed, downshifting. "It's all big estates. A lot of people just come out here on the weekends to ride their horses." She gestured at a cream-colored barn that looked bigger than their high school at home. "Uncle Thomas has one of the only working farms in this section. He says the county association is always calling, asking if he wants to sell, so they can break it up into estates."

Anna flicked on the turn signal and braked rapidly. Megan saw a stone pillar with a plaque set into it reading, "Given Farm." In front of them stretched a long gravel driveway, flanked by open pastures, which disappeared into trees up ahead.

"This is it," Anna said, turning into the drive. "Welcome home."

ABOUT THE AUTHOR

Emma Carlson Berne lives in Ohio with her husband, Aaron, and her son, Henry.

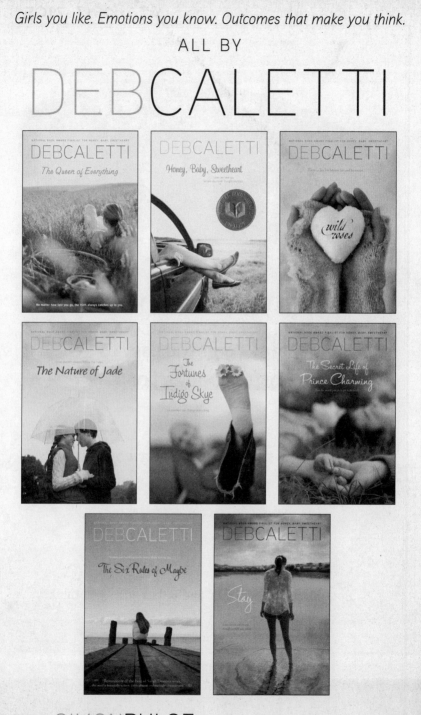